INTO THE
ROARING FORK

3/23/17

JEANNIE,

THANKS FOR THE DRINKS!

Jeff Howe

ISBN: 0692345876
ISBN 13: 9780692345870

"Jeff Howe's *Into the Roaring Fork* is a masterful thriller that chronicles the life of a Middlebury College graduate who gets into trouble in Aspen. It illustrates the fine line between being on the right or wrong side of the law, and the soul searching that occurs when one is in trouble. It's one of those books you will not be able to put down once you start reading." **- Santa J. Ono, President, University of Cincinnati**

"With his first book, Howe personally relates to life as a ski bum in his novel *Into the Roaring Fork*. Set in Aspen in 1985, the book is an unexpected tale of suspense and mystery in the local backcountry." **- Steamboat Today**

"In Jeff Howe's new book, *Into the Roaring Fork*, two Middlebury College grads take up ski bum jobs in Colorado but veer off onto a path that leads them into the darkness of the Rocky Mountains." **- Addison Independent**

"A suspenseful tale of ski bums and drugs in 1980s Aspen." **– Summit Daily News**

"*Into the Roaring Fork* captures the beauty and wonder of the Rocky Mountains and makes readers feel a part of the adventure. It is a thrilling story filled with love and deception that keeps readers on the edge of their seats." **– Crested Butte News**

"If you're into stuff by names like Patterson, Child or Connelly, then you will likely enjoy what Howe brings to the table. Into the Roaring Fork lacks the uber-badass lead character that some of the authors I mention tend to lean on to drive their action, but Howe is still going for that taut, stripped-down, breathless rollercoaster ride from the opening page until it all wraps up. He succeeds in many ways." – **Missoula Independent**

"Compact chapters, along with multiple storylines that race through memorable scenery, certainly help aid Howe's goal of writing a page-turner."
-Petoskey News

"Howe writes from the perspective of the main character, Alex Cavanaugh, a recent graduate set out for Aspen. Cavanaugh, however, finds himself traveling deeper into the dark and dangerous pathways of not only the mountains but also life itself. Life adventures made into a suspenseful fiction novel." – **UC Magazine**

"*Into the Roaring Fork* by Jeff Howe is a taut, fast-paced tale that's remarkably good for a first novel." – **Lansing State Journal**

"*Into the Roaring Fork* has the promise of a quality writer who has stories to tell. Read it." – **Lincoln Journal Star**

For Kathleen, Jackson, and Holland

CHAPTER ONE

His new 1985 blue-and-white Chevy Blazer came to a stop at the end of a remote, unmapped, dirt road deep within the Rocky Mountains. I got out of the passenger seat and walked around to the tailgate. Popped it open. I lifted the fully loaded backpack out of the rear of the four-wheel drive and flung it onto my back, slipping my arms through the shoulder straps and then buckling the hip belt. The snap of the plastic signaled *go* just like a green light. It felt heavier than the night before when I'd finished packing and thrown it on for a dress rehearsal. Morning, though, can add weight to anything.

He sat in the driver seat waiting for me. I leaned into the open front passenger window.

"Got everything you need?" he asked.

I adjusted the left shoulder strap and pulled the compass from my jeans just to double-check. "I'm good. It's all here."

"OK, see you in about thirty-six hours. Do everything just like last time, Alex, and we're golden."

"I'll be waiting right here for you," I replied. "And try not to forget the takeout this time."

I remembered how hungry I had gotten back in June. I was craving greasy food when I made it back to the road after the twenty-six-mile round-trip hike, and Carter had shown up empty-handed.

We shook hands, and he pulled away with a U-turn and headed back down the valley. A few feet from the trailhead I stopped and watched the four-wheel drive kick up a cloud of dust and disappear into it like a boat in thick fog. I was alone. I felt it. Same as last time. Equal parts good and bad, I let it all sink in until I knew my senses were on full alert. Then I got moving.

Mineral King was a rarely traveled trail. In the fall a few hunters used it, and occasionally a fisherman might attempt the trek to one of the trout streams in the area, but that was about it. Most people didn't even know it existed. Just a few locals. It had been around for a hundred years or so. Back in the days of the silver mines and lead mines they used mules to haul their quarry on it, and as I walked it I knew I really was doing nothing different than that relative of the horse.

I was heading west-southwest through the White River National Forest. Beginning in the Roaring Fork Watershed and then on to the southernmost point of another unpaved, backcountry, wilderness road. Then a few hundred yards beyond to Oar Lake, my destination. Lots of up and down. My boots impacting the dry, solid earth. Little round stones acting like ball bearings on the steep, downhill slopes on the trail. Evergreen branches were my banisters from time to time, keeping me upright like a father behind his little boy on skates. But my legs were strong. I felt strong. And I had quickly gotten over the first impression of the heavy backpack and the occasional nuisance of the loose gravel. I was moving, and the combination of a rising body temperature and the cool air made the going seem easy.

It was early July, two months after I had graduated from college. Summer in the mountains. A paradise. Back in mid-June—my first time on the trail—I'd had to worry about the possibility of snow up in the high elevations, which I feared, but now it was nonexistent. It would stay on the peaks far above me. The sun and blue sky above us all. A meandering trail weaved in and out of the conifers and aspens, valleys with flowers and streams and massive granite boulders transported by glaciers from another time. Everything so clear. Views never ending and reverential. I loved it all. This place had always been a part of my life. As a boy growing up in Arlington, Virginia, we cooled off in the Adirondacks during summer, and then eventually the

Rockies and Aspen as a teenager every July and August. There was nowhere I would rather be. And to be paid for being there was easy to say yes to, even knowing the risks. I could've hiked for a hundred miles had Carter asked, but he only needed me to do thirteen in and thirteen out. Two days. From the road to the lake and back.

CHAPTER TWO

We met senior year at Middlebury College. Taking a photography course, it just so happened I got the open seat next to her in the classroom. I signed up for the elective because I needed a few credits more to graduate. It seemed fairly painless. I'd be done by the end of May and on the road out west. She was an art major and this was a required part of her curriculum. I could tell she was prepared, with all the books, a few cameras, lenses, cases. She looked the part too: faded jeans, a black cotton sweater, and Doc Martens. A silver loop earring hanging from each ear and lots of bracelets on each wrist. The skin on her face, neck, and hands was tan. Her dark hair with caramel highlights was long and pulled back into a ponytail. She smiled at me. It was slightly crooked, which made it even more beautiful. She had either been born with perfectly straight white teeth or had braces. Her thick black eyebrows were Mediterranean, but her Windex-blue eyes said another world. A place I'd never been to.

"I'll buy you a beer if you lend me one of your cameras," I said to her.

She glanced over with that little crooked smile, her notepad and pen sitting on top of her desk.

"You don't have a camera?"

"No," I said, and grinned.

"So if you don't have a camera, do you even know how to use one?"

"I thought that's what I'd learn how to do in this class," I told her.

"You would if it was Intro to Photography. This one's a few levels above that."

"Well let's get back to the beer part," I suggested, knowing my amateur status in photography was fully revealed by then. She laughed.

I extended my hand to hers, and introduced myself. Her name was Erin. She was a senior too. On her way out. A studio art major with the potential of financial starvation upon graduation, but I don't think she ever worried about that. She was from Pacific Palisades in Los Angeles. Big homes overlooking the ocean. Her dad was high up at Occidental Petroleum. She started her college career at the Fashion Institute of Technology in Manhattan, but after a couple of years she realized that painting—oils and acrylics—was the direction she wanted to go. She was also ready to leave the city, but not the East Coast. Middlebury became her choice. She had checked it out at the request of her father, who was a distinguished member of its alumni, and she liked their program. Liked what she saw. The charming campus setting, with lots of grass and trees was a nice change of pace from Manhattan.

She took me up on my offer, and after a couple of weeks we were together all the time. We met each other's friends, went to class, made our rounds at all the parties, and jumped in bed every chance we got.

It was a winter with tons of snowfall. We took ski trips up to Killington and Stratton Mountain. Since she had begun skiing at age five, she had no problem keeping up with me. She kept her hands like a boxer's on the bumps. Upper body always square with the fall line. Mostly just her legs moving and knees absorbing the bumps. It was pretty to watch her. In Stratton we stayed at this little slope-side hotel, and she made me hot chocolate with Cointreau and peppermint schnapps. We drank it in bed. She tossed little marshmallows in my cup. Two at a time. Peanut butter and jelly squares cut up on a paper plate lay next to us and our clothes were scattered over the floor. Skis leaning up against a corner wall. Our boots still dripping melted snow.

She had a one-bedroom apartment on the second floor of a two-family house a block away from campus. It was really a two-bedroom, but she converted one of the rooms into her studio. A nice setup for a college kid. Much better than the five-bedroom house I shared with four other guys. Complete with an overflow of dirty dishes in the sink, moldy shower, and trashy furniture.

We spent most of our time together at her place. I eventually kept clothes there. They hung in the closet in her studio with her art supplies, canvases ready to be stretched, brushes, an extra easel, and a box of her old photos. On the room's wood floor was a painter's tarp with every color on it. Droplets of past works. Her easel stood in the center, angled to catch natural light from the window. A rectangular, red, four-legged table stood next to it. There were always paint tubes on it. Each one a different shape from being squeezed a certain way. A few untouched.

She painted the walls yellow. Her favorite color. One of her landscapes hung on them. A Beatles poster and a Dali print she'd picked up at the MOMA gift shop hanging across from it. Sometimes I'd sit in the corner on the purple beanbag chair stretched out with a magazine. I liked watching her paint. I'd put on records and be warmed by the music and sunlight. My foot periodically touched the bottom of the ancient radiator that amused us with its whistle. Air being sucked into the torpedo-shaped vent as the steam cooled, condensed into water, and flowed downstream.

A row of track lights hung from the ceiling and were trained on her easel and the work in progress. Her back to the lights, at night they cast moving shadows of her on the floor, her arm going back and forth from palette to canvas.

She worked hard. Her degree was being pursued. Mine was more about the finish line. After four years of college, I was ready to move on. The novelty of higher education had worn off, though I knew many of the friendships would be missed when everyone went their separate ways. So I absorbed what I could in the time I had left. My degree in economics was almost completed. I had loaded up on required courses my first three years, which made senior year somewhat easier. By winter it was just a matter of choosing electives to have enough credits to graduate in May.

Erin had been playing catch-up ever since she transferred to Middlebury and switched majors. She was determined though to remain with her peers and graduate on schedule. In four years like everyone else. Something about not being left behind pushed her.

Late nights in the studio became routine. Eventually she'd come to bed—usually, sometimes not. Sometimes I'd see her curled up in the beanbag chair in the morning with paint on her fingers and clothes. The lights would still be on, an empty glass of chocolate milk next to her on the floor. The ashtray. She'd hear me in the shower and wake up. The bathroom door would open, and her hand would hit the light switch. Total darkness and my laughter. I could hear hers. She would either come in and join me or wait for me to get out. After three months the sex was still amazing. Every way. Every place.

CHAPTER THREE

By ten o'clock I had made it all the way to Silver Creek. I was ahead of schedule. Twenty minutes faster than my trip in June. The stream was low and clear. Gin clear. No rain in almost two weeks. Brook trout rising and sipping pupil-size caddis flies on the surface. I was tempted to unpack my four-piece fly rod from the brown aluminum tube it was in, but that would not be sticking to the plan. The rod and reel were simply a decoy. An excuse if I needed one. Everything had to be done just like last time. I kept hearing his words.

I took my backpack off, laid it down on the rocks, and pulled out one of my bottles of water while taking a seat by the creek. Even though I wasn't overly thirsty, I knew the importance of keeping hydrated and resting. A tired body and mind can make mistakes. A broken ankle or even a bad sprain can be fatal when you're miles and miles from anyone. I drank half the bottle, ate some M&M's, and then drank the rest while watching those fish: the beauty of the thin white stripe on the bottom of their fins.

After a few minutes I got up and unhooked the water purifier that was attached with a bungee cord to the outside frame of the backpack. I used it to pump purified Silver Creek water into the empty bottle. Giardia was another concern. Even the clearest mountain water can harbor it. I took precautions.

The sun was now higher in the mountain sky, slowly rising like the trout. The temperature climbed with it. At the edge of the creek I took off my hiking boots, stuffed my wool socks into them, and tossed them twenty feet across the water to the rocks on the opposite bank. Dry shoes and feet were a priority. My jeans were replaced with shorts. With my backpack securely fastened to my body, I carefully waded into the water below the pool where the trout were feeding. It was shallower there: knee-high. The current picked up with each step, but it posed little threat of sweeping me off my feet. Still, I took my time, avoiding the pointed stones in the streambed, feeling for them with my toes. A few spots were painful, but I was being paid a boatload of money. It made me smile. A way to counter the bruising on my soles.

On the other side I grabbed my boots and sat down to put them on. Taking my time while my feet dried on the warm rocks and sunlight. One of the boots had land-ed next to a piece of clear plastic wrapper. Remnants of a packet of sunflower seeds. It surprised me to see that someone had recently been there, but even more it made me upset that some fisherman would spoil the remoteness and beauty of the location with such a careless disposal of trash. I picked it up and put it in my pocket. My good deed.

The trail became faint beyond Silver Creek. Harder to read. Much less travelled than the even rarely used sec-tion I'd already covered that day. And it grew steep. Just the mountain animals' occasional usage keeping it trod-den enough to even call it a trail. I shortened my steps. Pacing myself. Methodically moving my arms and legs like a member of a marching band. Ascending into the higher elevations. Struggling at times to read the trail and to even stay on it. Periodically checking my compass. Looking for familiar boulders, or trees that I had remembered being snapped by an avalanche or burned by lightning. It was a long way up to the pass. This was one of the most tir-ing sections of the trail. One foot in front of the other. Soldiering on, up beyond the tree line where the land-scape was windswept and seemingly barren.

When I reached the pass, I pulled out my binocu-lars to scan the horizon and the valleys. The one I had come from and the one I was headed for. It was easy to see things above the tree line, but below that not much could be seen. It didn't worry me though. The probability of running into a ranger at this point was low. I was too far in for them to come on foot, and the horse trails they used mainly for forest fire prevention were south of me. I was halfway there. A beautiful day in the mountains.

Standing there, I took it all in. Thought about everything I was doing. My life had changed so quickly. A few months back I was just finishing up school. And now I was miles from the rest of the world. Alone. Taking big risks. Ones that could result in the loss of my freedom. My future. Decisions I made and contemplated. I had made the choice to be there. That in itself was empowering. The consequences and rewards had been weighed. I was breathing heavily at eleven thousand feet and had never felt more alive. I had reached the halfway point in, and I realized that in a way I had done the same with my life.

CHAPTER FOUR

F or the second time that Friday evening, they drove by
the restaurant and counted the cars in the once full
parking lot. It was later now, and the vehicles had dwindled
down to six, same as the number of rounds chambered
in Lowell Henderson's .357. He noted the faintly illuminated red Isuzu Trooper still in the space closest to the
entrance, and continued on Donner Pass Road for a quar-
ter mile to Bridge Street. He took a right and traversed
the railroad tracks and the raging Truckee River, and
took another right on South Meadow. A thousand feet of
pavement for residential access turned into dirt and gravel
that paralleled the Truckee for seven miles—halfway to
Lake Tahoe. Lowell had driven it earlier in the day without

encountering anyone. The campers, anglers, and rafters were still a month away from arriving in earnest because of the impact of the spring thaw on the river, which made it much too high and muddy to fish or float. That was why he had chosen to be there in late April: he knew they'd be without company then.

Bouncing along with their high beams on, they came to the spot that Lowell had scouted and marked with a whitewall tire he had found on the riverbank that afternoon. He pulled the grey pickup with the matching truck cap into the turnout and put it in park.

He and Kaylee got out and walked the area with their flashlights. When they were certain it was vacant, he used a screwdriver to remove his registered license plates, stow them in the bed, and then put stolen ones on. Back to the restaurant in the quieting town of Truckee they drove, where they parked nearby on the street and waited. When the number of cars—including the Isuzu—had whittled down to two, Lowell gave final instructions to Kaylee and exited the vehicle. He walked across the dark lot and entered the thin strip of brush that separated the eatery from the river. He was invisible there.

At 11:30 pm the assistant manager walked out the front door and got into the Honda Accord that was midway down the left side of the parking lot. He drove away, going right past Kaylee who was laying low in the pickup. Ten minutes later the lights inside the restaurant went out, and the proprietor locked the front door and walked to his car holding a brown vinyl money pouch that was zippered shut. A few steps and he was there. He opened the Isuzu's door, and as he took a seat behind the wheel, a man in a dark denim jacket and black leather gloves pointing a revolver at him appeared in the front passenger window.

"Open the door now," Lowell demanded. Clayton Binns, in complete shock leaned over and flipped the lock. Lowell got in. "Back out and take a right on Donner Pass."

The proprietor had the keys in his left hand and they began to jingle as he started shaking. With his other hand, he picked up the money bag seated between them and attempted to hand it to Lowell. "Just take the money and go," the man said as he looked Lowell in the eyes while the interior light began to dim. He had hoped to find some amount of mercy in them, but there was nothing, just the pupils that were as dark as the hair that fell over the ears and framed the face.

"Put the pouch back down, put the keys in the ignition, and don't ever tell me what to do again." Lowell put the gun to the man's temple.

The Isuzu started up and backed out. "Go right on Donner Pass." Lowell instructed. They drove by Kaylee and she followed. "Take a right on Bridge," he ordered.

Clayton did as Lowell told him. When they made it to the bumpy dirt road, Lowell cocked the hammer of the gun. Sweat began pouring down the man's face and Lowell could see it in slivers of light that were reflecting in the rear view mirror from the pickup behind them.

"Oh, my god! Don't shoot me, mister," he pleaded as they pitched and tossed and turned on their way further into the forest along the Truckee.

"Didn't I tell you not to tell me what to do?"

"I'm sorry. I didn't mean it. I just don't want that gun to go off." It was planted into the side of Clayton's head and he could feel the end of the barrel moving up and down and sideways like a crayon in a child's hand as the four-wheel drive was put to work on the riddled terrain. A slight bump moved it a half inch. A big one, double that.

"I accept your apology. As for the gun going off, that's up to you. If you're a good driver, then we'll have a smooth ride and nothing will jerk my trigger finger. If you're care-less, well that could result in a different outcome."

"I'm driving the best I can. I promise."

He continued as though the man hadn't spoken. "It's totally up to you. Even though the gun is in my hands, you hold your life in your own," Lowell told him without a hint of emotion; he had less feeling for the man than the sur-face area of the barrel tip connected to his head.

Clayton fell silent, and continued focusing on driving, which felt like a tightrope he was walking. When Lowell saw the whitewall tire, he instructed him to steer the car into the turnout. "Put it in park and shut down the mo-tor." Kaylee pulled in behind them with her high beams on. Without taking his gun and eyes off the driver, Lowell picked up the vinyl pouch, opened the door, and got out of the Isuzu. Kaylee arrived quickly at his side and he handed the pouch to her. She then left to deposit the money in their pickup. "Take the keys from the ignition and place them on my seat," he told the man. After the proprietor placed them there and returned to his fully-upright position behind the wheel, Lowell picked them up and slid them into his gray corduroy pants pocket. "Now exit the vehicle here on my side."

Clayton didn't want to leave his car. "I'm not telling you what to do, I'm asking, okay. Can you please just take the money and leave me be?"

Lowell stood with a grip on the opened door. "I need you to step outside the vehicle. I won't ask you again." The gun trained on the man's midsection for the highest percentage shot if needed.

The restaurant proprietor stepped out into the spotlight of the high beams. Lowell instructed him to walk toward the lights and take center stage between the front and rear of the two vehicles. Kaylee and Lowell corralled him there, their revolvers taking aim. She used a two-handed grip. Lowell, only one. The balding middle-aged man voluntarily put his shaking hands above his head, bringing them together as in prayer to control them, but it had little effect.

"When I was in prison," Lowell began, "I could see the warden's car from my cell window. He had a reserved space right by the entrance to the administration building. All I had to do was look between the bars to see whether or not I was in the pleasure of his company. Any of this sound familiar to you?"

"No," the man replied as he began lowering his arms.

"Did I tell you to bring your hands down?"

"I'm sorry." The hands rose.

"Did I tell you to put them up?"

"No, you didn't." Clayton paused. "Please, I'm sorry. I'm not trying to cause any trouble. I don't know what you want me to do." The voice and the man sounded on the verge of breaking down.

"*Don't know what to do?* That doesn't sound like a guy who parks his car in the head honcho's space every time he pulls into work." Lowell took a step into the light, the man facing him. "Driving past your restaurant these last few days, I saw your Isuzu right there by the front door each time. I guess you're like the warden, aren't you?"

Before the man could reply, Kaylee came forward and cocked the hammer on her .38; a present from Lowell two years prior when she turned thirty five. It was unmarked, which he paid extra for on the black market. Clayton Binns heard the mechanized sound of impending doom and turned its direction. It was the first time he'd gotten a good look at her. It surprised him how much she resembled his typical female customer, which for the last three days she had been in order to surveil the restaurant and its owner. A woman in her mid-to-late thirties who saw to keeping herself fit and trim, with shoulder-length hair the color of a stream after heavy rains. Not only was she the type he commonly observed at his place of business, but in all of the Northern Sierras as well.

"I'm begging you not to take my life," he said to her.

"Can I shoot him?" she asked Lowell, her two crooked upper incisors on full display as she smiled, which she didn't do often because of them.

"I'm begging you, please don't." He dropped to his knees.

Lowell let him anguish for a few moments and then approached him. "Today's you're lucky day, Warden. You've got about a two-mile walk back to town. Take it nice and slow and that'll give us plenty of time to be on our way. Okay?"

"Okay, I promise."

Lowell and Kaylee got into the pickup and drove away.

The night was black without the lights. Clayton Binns noticed the darkness but wept for joy. He would see his wife and children once again, after having lived through those unbearable moments when he thought he never would. He regained his composure and found his courage and his desire for justice; fueled by hate and anger for the assailants who robbed him and mercilessly administered a brand of mental torture that was far more painful than the loss of money. With only the crescent moon to guide him, he began running. The road was littered with potholes, so he had to tread carefully through the minefield. He did just that, and with his determination he managed to cover a mile in under ten minutes. Another ten and he'd be calling the police. He became sweaty and took off his blue windbreaker, discarding it on the road where it followed a big bend in the river. As it straightened out, Lowell suddenly appeared from the shadows. He shined his flashlight on the proprietor and the man came to an abrupt stop in his street shoes, khakis, and cowboy shirt. The same beads of sweat dripping down his face that Lowell had seen earlier in the Isuzu.

"I knew you'd come running, Warden."

He fired one shot point blank into the man's abdomen. It sent him to the ground. The second shot to the forehead put him below it.

CHAPTER FIVE

Kerrigan walked down the hallway and went into Lamar's office. "Looks like we've got another one. Gayle's on line four."

Lamar pressed the button on the phone and the one on the speaker. "What do you have for us, Gayle?"

"Male, Caucasian, forty nine, one shot to the stomach, one to the head. The body was discovered by a search team in a wooded area one mile outside the town of Truckee, California."

"Where's Truckee?" Lamar asked Kerrigan.

"Lake Tahoe."

"Okay, continue on, Gayle."

"Victim was identified as Clayton Binns, the owner of *Clay's*, a restaurant in Truckee. Married, father of two."

There was a brief pause as the news hit home—each of theirs, where their own children and spouses would be waiting to greet them after work.

"When will the ballistics be ready?" Lamar asked her.

"I should have something later today."

"Alright, let's talk then."

"I'm getting the full report ready and will have that for you later as well."

They ended the call and Kerrigan took a seat across from Lamar's desk. "Sounds like our boy."

"Boys," Lamar said correcting him. "It's definitely two. I'm sure they'll come back with a second set of tire prints like the others."

"But that doesn't necessarily mean there's two of them. I still think there's the possibility he parks his car off the beaten path and then huffs it. He waits for the restaurant to close, comes up behind the guy and then forces him to give him a lift back to his car. Bang, bang, and off he goes. Each victim has been found within two miles of their restaurant."

"It's possible, but I still think there are two of them." Lamar turned and looked at the map of the United States on his wall. "They claim their first victim here in Phoenix and—"

"I wouldn't exactly call Mesa, Phoenix," Kerrigan jumped in.

"Call it what you want. Mesa it is. Then Bend, Oregon, and now Tahoe." He stood up to get a closer look at things."

"You really think two guys are going to travel thousands of miles to steal a few grand?"

"That's just it, I don't. And I don't think one guy would do it either. Which leads me to believe it's not just the money."

Kerrigan thought about what Lamar was implying. "You thinking he's just an executioner and getting his jollies by dragging off townies in the middle of the night?"

"*Just* an executioner."

"You know what I mean." Kerrigan got up from the chair and took a file on the case from Lamar's desk before heading back to his office. At the doorway, he paused. "I'm going to the range at noon. Maybe I'll see you there."

CHAPTER SIX

We flew to Los Angeles for spring break. Our school friends were highly disappointed. They headed down to Fort Lauderdale and were expecting us to ride along. The last hurrah. But both of us had done the Florida spring break scene before, her parents had offered to pay plane tickets, and LA sounded fun. I had never been there, and I knew she wanted me to meet her parents. Things had gotten serious.

Her parents met us at LAX and drove us to their place in Pacific Palisades. It was even nicer than I expected. Erin's father did well at Occidental Petroleum, but her mother also had money from her side of the family. Their large home overlooked the Pacific. An incredible view.

The pool, the manicured lawn, and the ocean all the way out to where the sky began.

We didn't stick around long. It was Friday, and a lot of her friends were in town. She felt a little guilty leaving her parents so quickly, but we'd be doing the dinner thing with them the next night. She wanted to show me around. Hang out with her friends. A few people were meeting for happy hour at Yesterday's in Westwood, which was just down the street from UCLA. We drove over that way. She took me through Beverly Hills and we did the obligatory drive-by of the *Beverly Hillbillies* house. Visited Marilyn Monroe's final resting place. Had a couple beers at the Polo Lounge. Sunshine everywhere. It felt good. It was the good life for sure.

We got to the bar a little late. Her friends had been waiting for us. They had a table with pitchers of beer on it and a couple of chairs reserved for us. She introduced me to everyone and I sat down next to her and Carter Pate.

"Let me pour you a beer, and here's a little something for later," he said, reaching for my hand and putting a small packet in it.

I glanced at it and put it in my pocket. It was a folded-up magazine paper that fit into the palm of my hand. I knew right away it was a gram of cocaine. Coke had become widespread, and the recreational use of it—on and off campus—was common.

"Thanks, Carter," I told him.

"Welcome to LA," he replied.

"Erin said it's a great place."

"It is, and any friend of Erin's is a friend of mine. Good to have you here."

At a hundred bucks a gram, his generosity went above and beyond, and I truly appreciated it. But doing blow wasn't my thing. It never did much for me. I had better chemistry with a few Rolling Rocks and a hit from a joint. Erin though, liked the stuff. I whispered to her what had just taken place and she reached under the table and put her hand on my crotch.

"Save some for me," she whispered back.

Carter was at least ten years older than everyone else at the table. He had graduated from Pomona College back in '74. He had a job. His tie was still on. I wasn't sure exactly what he did, but he must've been doing well. Erin said he was a business owner and dabbled in a few other things. She didn't know all that much about him, but he had been dating her best friend, Kelley Alston, for about a year. Kelley confided to Erin that he could be "the one." They had met at a party through a mutual friend. Kelley was finishing up school like us and wanted to move in with him when she graduated from Pepperdine.

Since he was sitting next to me and it was hard to hear or talk to the others, I really only had the chance to get to know Carter. Music and the crowd filtered out other conversations, like Erin and Kelley catching up.

"So I heard you and Erin are launching into the real world soon," said Carter.

"I'm ready. Definitely ready. But maybe not the nine-to-five thing yet."

"What are your plans?"

"I'm going to try my best to talk Erin into moving out to Colorado to ski for a year," I replied.

"Oh yeah, what town?"

"Aspen."

"Good choice. Best mountain town in the Rockies."

"Do you ski there?" I asked him.

"I do, but I like it even better there now in the summer. I bought a place there last year and really got into all the stuff you can do once the snow melts. The Roaring Fork River is right out my back door, and I took up fly-fishing."

"Glad to hear I'm sitting next to a fellow angler. I fly-fish too. The Roaring Fork is one of the best in Colorado. I'm jealous," I said. And I truly was. I could only dream of having that water steps away from my home. A second home at that.

"I'm still a rookie, so referring to me as an angler might not be appropriate just yet. Hey, you and Erin are more than welcome to use my place as a starting point if you do make it out. You can show me the ropes."

"Carter, you are too kind. And thanks again for my little welcome package," I said.

"No problem. Enjoy it."

We stayed at the bar for a couple hours, and during that time I found out that Carter and I had a few things in common. We were both skiers, loved the mountains, went to Outward Bound in our teens, dated best friends, and Aspen was held in high esteem. I really liked him. It was easy to become his friend, and I could see why Kelley was into him.

The four of us went out to his car and found a little side street off Wilshire where we parked and he cut up lines of coke for his passengers. He had plenty of it. He put it on a small mirror and passed it around. From there we drove over to Santa Monica and met up with everyone again at a dive bar. It was Erin and Kelley's choice. A favorite of theirs. One of the first places they were able to buy beers when they were in high school. They never carded. Cheap beers and peanut shells on the floor.

We all stood around the bar, which gave me the opportunity to talk with some of Erin's other friends. I got the impression there wasn't a bad apple in the bunch. It made for a pleasant evening.

When Erin came up to me and asked me to get her a beer and a pack of matches from the bartender so she could light her cigarette, we had a moment to ourselves.

"I'm glad you talked me into coming to LA," I said to Erin.

"I told you it would be fun," she replied, her eyes full of happiness.

"Your friends are great, and did you know that Carter has a place in Aspen?" I was planting the seed.

"Kelley told me about it last year. She's been there with him. He also has a plane and can fly it there," she said.

"Does he fly the plane himself? Is he a pilot?" I was ready to hold him in even higher regard if the answer was yes. I had always loved planes. To be able to go anywhere, anytime. The freedom of flight.

"Yeah, she flew with him."

Later that night we went back to Westwood for a party. Someone knew someone who went to UCLA. There were tons of people. The four of us stuck together and I got to know a little more about Carter. He was thirty-four, though the five o'clock shadow and dimpled chin made him look younger. No doubt he was a good-looking guy. Medium height and slightly on the slender side, but well toned. He had short, wavy blond hair and green eyes. With a cowboy hat and giving up a few inches, he could pass for Butch Cassidy.

"So what's your recipe for success?" I asked him when I returned with two beers from an ice-filled tub and handed him one.

"Recipes. I'm in the restaurant business."

He went on to explain that he owned six of them, and a few bars. All of them in LA.

"A quick ascent to the top." I was impressed with what he'd accomplished at his young age. "Cheers."

"Well, I've been at it for a while."

"How long?"

"Since junior year at Pomona when I took out a loan from my Dad to buy a sub shop right next to campus. So I'm definitely not some overnight success," he said modestly.

I could tell he would rather talk about something else, so I did. "I heard you like flying."

That was his passion and he lit up at the subject. "I learned to fly before I learned to drive. My dad was a naval pilot in WWTwo, and he taught me."

His plane was a twin engine. It could fly nonstop to Aspen from LA. Flying into and out of the mountains kept him on his toes, which he liked. That was the fun of it.

We eventually made it back to Erin's car. Said our good-byes to Carter and Kelley, and drove to Erin's house. It was well past midnight. I just wanted to sit outside on their back lawn and listen to the ocean. We grabbed a reclining lounge chair from the pool. Both of us lying on it. She was on her side with her leg over mine. Her head on my chest.

"Did you have fun tonight?" she asked.

"It was awesome. I'm so glad we didn't go to Lauderdale."

"We made the right call. And I really wanted you to meet my parents and friends."

"Everything and everyone has been great," I told her.

"My mom thinks you're handsome," Erin said, lifting her head up to look at me.

"Is she going to sneak up to my room later?" Her fingernails dug into my side. "Just kidding, just kidding," I began to plead as she applied more and more pressure. I grabbed her and lifted her on top of me. She sat up and straddled my hips. The pool lights glowing on her face and hair. Her white linen shirt. "Hey, I want to ask you something," I said.

"What?" she replied.

I took my hands and slid them under her shirt, and then she began to unbutton it for me. When she finished, she unclasped her bra. She leaned forward. Her outstretched arms braced on my chest. "I'm still waiting," she said seductively, and she took out her ponytail and let her hair drape across my face. The breeze coming off the Pacific catching strands of it.

"Let's move to Aspen when we graduate."

"And be like boyfriend and girlfriend and live together," she said without hesitation. Her crooked smile came alive on her face. She loved playing with me.

"Just trying to make all your dreams come true," I said.

"Likewise." She got up and took off all her clothes. She was so amazing looking.

I grabbed a beach towel from the chair next to us and spread it out on the lawn. I laid her down on it. Quiet. Everyone inside asleep. Just the sound of our bodies.

CHAPTER SEVEN

I learned to use a compass when I went to Outward Bound during the summer of my sophomore year in high school. I thought it was an amazing instrument. They taught us how to use it in conjunction with a map and how to use it alone. We had to learn how to take bearings and make our way to a designated place. Adjust the compass housing. "Put the red in the shed." It was clear to me. Came easy.

My first test was near the Appalachian Trail in Maine. We used the trail to hike up to a clearing. In the distance down below we saw Bald Mountain Pond. A small lake three miles away. We then had to make our way to the lake without using the trail. I pulled out my compass. Held it in the palm of my hand in front of my chest. I took a bearing. Used my instrument, and off I went. The thick forest left me blind to the lake as I descended. I stopped every minute or so to look at the compass. Held it still. Made sure I was going the right way. Then continued on.

That day, I passed the test. Harder ones followed. They ran through my mind as I worked my way down from the pass high up in the Rockies and into the valley. The trail was so hard to read. I couldn't figure out why it was so much tougher than when I was on it only a couple weeks prior back in June. Maybe the drought. I stopped again and again to recheck my compass. It didn't seem right. I knew I might have to make adjustments for the magnetic declination, but even with that I was hesitant with my direction of travel in relation to the sun.

I stopped. I took off my backpack and walked a few feet away from it. Down the mountain. I wanted to make sure there wasn't anything metal interfering with the compass needle. I took off my belt as well. I turned my back to the sun, which meant I had to be facing north. The first lesson for bearings in the northern hemisphere. The needle wasn't pointing in the opposite direction. It was off forty degrees. That was too much. I pulled out my water bottle. I sat down on the slope. I thought about the landmarks that I had noticed. I had crossed Silver Creek. I knew that I couldn't be too far off the trail, if I was even off it at all. And I had made it to the pass. But I began to question if it was the right pass. Was it even a pass at all? It had looked familiar, but then I thought maybe it didn't.

The compass worried me a little. I always trusted it. Couldn't figure out how I broke it. Why it wasn't working. I drank my water and sat there. The sun still high in the Colorado sky. Cotton ball clouds slowly sailing by. It was a peaceful and quiet setting. I grabbed a peanut butter and jelly sandwich which was double wrapped and water-proofed like everything else. By the third or fourth bite it came to me: I was near some of the old lead and silver mines. They were certainly capable of producing false readings on my compass. It made sense. After all, that's what the trail was originally used for a hundred years ago. I told myself to be more diligent. Something like that shouldn't have been overlooked, and that upset me. I had been careless. There was no margin for error. No room for mistakes. Every mistake had a consequence, and mine would be no exception. Those were the rules.

If I was in the mining areas, then I had drifted too far south. I knew this from the map. I would have to use the sun to get back on course. Travel north. I thought about going back up above the tree line. Find a peak to use as a marker, a bearing, but that would take an extra hour. I figured I could just use the sun to make it to Wilson Creek. I would be out of the mining area there. The compass would be working again. Simply head west for a few miles, and I would meet up with him. He would be waiting for me. Everyone had agreed to a three-hour window for either of us. Plenty of time just in case something had gone wrong. A delay, a late start, an injury, or a trail hard to read.

My spirits were lifted, and I continued downward into the valley and toward the creek. I would find it. It ran the entire length of the valley floor. Keep going down and run right into it eventually. My pace quickened. Legs and feet planting firmly with each step. The food and water giving me fuel to burn. The weight on my back not a factor. Some of the rocks I could hop on, over, and off of. Slide a foot or two on the landing. Grab a tree to slow myself down when needed. The pine bark rough on my hands. Moving in and out of the beams of sunlight that pierced the woods. Sunlight that became less and less the lower I went.

Keep moving. My words to myself. Forehead wiped with an old bandana. Never stopping. I was traveling with a sense of urgency. I knew I was keeping an ever-growing sense of fear at bay with the pace I had set. Figuring the physical world around me would require all my attention. Not give my mind a chance to go places I knew it was capable of going. Stay busy. Swift travels.

I had never been lost before. I had always been able to follow a trail. Any trail. I had been on this same trail doing the same thing not long ago. Got in and got out. No problems. I just wasn't paying as close attention this time. Took things for granted. The pretty day. Possible scenarios forgone for the elk on the distant slope, the eagle, the trout rising. I had enjoyed myself too much. Instead I should've been more focused and checking the compass more often. What would I say to the ranger if our paths crossed? What if for some strange reason he wanted to check the backpack? Could I get my fishing license out easily if he asked to see it? All these things that were so important and should've been continuously rehearsed in my mind. They had become secondary because of the success of my last trip. And now I had to face the fact that I had gotten lost in the middle of a huge national forest. Accept it and remain calm. Get back on track. Quickly, but not carelessly.

The terrain began to level off, and I knew the creek had to be near. Aspen trees became more mixed in with the evergreens. I was being more observant. I stopped and checked my compass. The needle pointed north, the opposite direction of the sun, which I could barely make out behind the clouds. It was a good feeling to know my valued instrument, which had earned my trust for so many years, was working again. The mines were behind me. I looked at my map. The creek had to be ahead of me if I just continued going northwest. I was too low to get a bearing, so I focused on the farthest tree I could see and walked toward it. My compass in the palm of my hand. Reach the tree and repeat the process.

I was only behind schedule by an hour at the most. Well within the window. I slowed down. A clearing just ahead. It was small but amazingly beautiful. Almost perfectly circular. The sun came out just as I reached it. A good place to stop and replenish the fluids in my body. Grass and yellow wildflowers blanketed the meadow. Waist high. A large rock the size and shape of a VW Bug. The only rock in the meadow—carried there thousands of years ago by some glacier. Impossible to pass up. Like an invitation from God. I walked over to it, took off my backpack, and climbed up on it while holding my water bottle.

A very small lake, or what could've been a pond, came into view. The reason for the clearing. Hidden in summer by the shoots of grasses and long-stemmed blossoms. I climbed back down to get my map out of the backpack. I couldn't recall seeing the lake on the map. Maybe it was too small to have even been noted. I was hoping to identify it though and get a more exact idea of where I was. As I reached for the pocket that contained the map, I noticed some letters and numbers lightly carved into the rock just a foot or two away from my backpack. The wind had moved the grass just enough for me to see it. When I took a closer look, it read "SEVANS" with a few random letters and numbers after it. It was poorly written. More scratched than carved. Like a product of kindergarten. It seemed fairly recent. Not worn. Still unpolished by rains and wind. It was very strange, and I stood there and just kept looking at it for a minute. I couldn't figure out what it meant. But I took it as a reminder to travel carefully. Be smart. Plant feet firmly. An injury to my legs, ankles, or feet could have life-threatening consequences. I didn't want to be carving my own name into a stone.

The lake wasn't on the map. Too small. A secret of the mountains. I walked around it and then continued heading northwest. There looked to be a trail. The grass had been flattened. A route for animals to and from the water. I followed it. I exited the clearing and began weaving between the trees. Rocks and dry dirt. I was still on the trail, as faint as it was, and it was continuing northwest.

Soon I heard water. Most likely Wilson Creek in the distance. I was moving toward it. Downwind. Sound carrying like leaves in autumn. Each step making it more easily defined. There were two big boulders that I passed and then a small lip I began to rise up on. The trail ended there, and I stopped. I froze. My heart began pounding like it never had before. Like it was trying to kick its way out of my chest. I couldn't believe what I was looking at. I blinked to check my eyes, which confirmed that I was wide awake and what was happening was real. Hauntingly real.

CHAPTER EIGHT

The end of our college careers approached quickly. The shorts and T-shirts all the students were wearing again was an imminent sign of the finish line just up ahead. Erin scrambled to complete all her projects. She was painting all the time. Missing out on the sunshine and the green world enveloping us. Always in her studio or the studios at school. I left her alone. She was jealous of my freedom and my easy schedule. I spent a lot of time with my friends. Somewhat reverting back to the parties and bar scene. Took a part-time job with the admissions department at the university. A paper shuffler. I had a couple finals approaching, but that was it.

I moved into Erin's place. What little I had, or wanted to keep was already there. I left my single bed at the house. Someone could find use for it. An old dresser too. Clothes, a few books, stereo, albums, posters, and fly rods came with me. It fit easily into her apartment. *Our place.* The first time either of us had lived with someone we called our boyfriend or girlfriend. When I unloaded the last of my clothes, she came home from the studio and made me dinner. Spaghetti. It had this sausage in it that was so good. A bottle of wine for her. Rolling Rock for me. Salad and garlic bread. We smoked a joint in the kitchen. With a chef's hat on top, she had on an apron her mom had bought for her in Europe. It had a picture of the Eiffel Tower. Going from the oven to the stove and counter, she'd stop and take a hit. We smoked half of it.

Dinner was served in the dining room. We sat at the little table by the window. She lit the candle. It was dusk, and we kept the lights off. Just the candle.

"To our first night together," she toasted.

"To many, many more."

"How about forever?" she said.

"That's what I meant to say."

She smiled and I smiled back. We were in love; maybe the first time truly for both of us. It just kept progressing, getting better and better. Some of it was timing. We were seniors with different outlooks than we had as freshmen. It was the end of school and a new beginning. Like us.

We talked about graduation. Her parents and my parents were coming into town for it. We wanted them to meet. We'd all go out to dinner maybe. Have some drinks. Put our best foot forward. We were pretty certain things would go smoothly. Our parents were similar. Hardworking and successful. Most likely traveled in the same circles in different parts of the country. They would have things in common. Conversation without needing much effort.

As we talked about the things to come, I wanted to make sure her decision to go with me to Colorado wasn't something she would regret later on. The mountains were my choice. She was my choice, and I was hers. But our destination was a detour from her original plan. LA was home for her. It was a place to pursue her career as an artist. She was connected there. It was the next step for her, there or New York City, and it would be a confirmation of all the late nights and deadlines she'd met in school.

I took a sip of my beer and put it back down on the table.

"Are you sure about Colorado?" I asked, looking into her eyes. Such a beautiful girl. So fun and so full of life. And she was willing to put me first. I only loved her more because of it and felt guilty for not putting her first.

"I'm sure about us," she said sincerely.

"I really love you."

"I love you too."

She reached over for my hand.

"I feel a little guilty about all this. I feel like you're doing much more for me than I am for you," I said.

"Hey, if you were trying to drag me to Fargo, then I'd be thinking a little differently. I think Aspen will be cool, and like you promised, it's only for one ski season. I can paint there, and we'll get jobs, ski passes, and have our own little place. Don't feel bad."

"After Aspen we'll move to LA, or wherever you want to go."

She leaned across the table and just before kissing me, whispered, "Paybacks are hell."

CHAPTER NINE

For three days they cased the First Federal Bank in Ogden, Utah. The manager, Mark Dempsey, was the first to arrive each morning at eight, and then the other employees began to filter in around eight forty-five. The one-story-red-brick building was an island in a sea of asphalt. There were two large picture windows and a steel-framed glass door facing the street, and each side had three windows. One for each office. The rear was windowless with just a steel door. Bordering the property was a furniture store, a bar, and a diner across the street. That's where they took turns eating to scout the bank. Each day the bank started seeing a steady flow of customers not long after opening at nine. There was no security guard. A police cruiser drove by each day at 11:00 a.m. and 2:00 p.m. The manager ate his lunch at the diner on two of the days, never wanting to stray too far from the bank, model employee that he was. On the second day, his wife joined him. She was pretty. A brunette. Good figure. She was in her early forties but looked much younger. She had the chicken salad.

On the third day, Lowell waited in his pickup out in the diner parking lot after finishing his late-afternoon meal. It wouldn't be long until the bank closed at five o'clock, the manager always being the last to leave around five thirty and locking the door behind him. Lowell watched him get into his Buick and then followed him. It was only three miles from the bank to his house. Lowell kept his distance.

It was a nice neighborhood. Nice house. Gray, cedar shake, three-bedroom colonial. Black shutters. Detached garage. Mark Dempsey, manager of First Federal Bank, pulled into the driveway, which was lined with white pines for privacy. Lowell noted the address, the absence of kids' toys in the yard, and kept driving with the windows down in the late-May sunshine. He drove all through the neighborhood, getting a good look at the area, and then he took the highway north out of town to the campground that was their temporary home.

The two of them sat outside their tent on a fallen aspen tree trunk. Early evening. Sun heading down behind the foothills that tightened the daylight like an image in a kaleidoscope. A fire pit ringed with rounded creek stones

the size and smoothness of turtle shells. The nearest campers fifty yards away in their RV.

"I followed him home. We'll do it tomorrow."

CHAPTER TEN

It was an amazing feeling to be on the road headed west. Erin next to me with her feet up on the dashboard. Windows down. Radio up. The dial constantly turning in Erin's quest for AM's national news and the stories she was following, and my choice for music on the FM stations. We had her Jeep Cherokee completely filled with all of our stuff. The rearview mirror useless. Road map between us. Diplomas packed somewhere in the duffel bags. Clothes crammed into big, green, plastic garbage bags and stuffed to the ceiling. Erin's easels stretching to the center console from the tailgate. Cardboard boxes for her brushes and paints. Just the stuff we needed. Nothing else. The furniture had all been given away. A few pieces we sold. She shipped most of her paintings home. Pots, plates, pans, and some silverware wrapped up in newspaper and boxed. Our stereos and records the same way. Whatever else we would need we planned to pick up in Colorado.

We took a lot of back roads. County highways. Seeing places for the first time. There was no hurry to get anywhere. I felt incredibly happy. It was how college was supposed to end, and the way life after school was to begin. The two of us and the rest of the world to explore.

We stopped off at Skaneateles Lake. One of the Finger Lakes in New York. Our first day on the road. It was just for a swim. Erin dared me to go in. She bet I wouldn't last more than two minutes. She knew how cold that water could be in early summer.

"And what do I get if I win?" I asked her.

"Me," she answered while holding an elastic band with her teeth as she arched her back and ran her hands through her hair to place it in a ponytail.

A friend of her parents had a cottage there. Erin knew exactly where it was from all the summers she had spent on that lake. She was born in Connecticut and lived there for twelve years before moving to LA when her dad was recruited by Occidental. For a few weeks every summer her parents rented the place next door to their friend's place. Both were a few doors down from Roosevelt Hall. The large Greek Revival home that a distant cousin of the two presidents, Franklin and

Theodore, had once owned and so aptly named. We pulled in. She knew they wouldn't be there this early in the season. Nobody was there at the lake yet. She grabbed a towel, and we walked around back to their boat dock. The moment of truth. At the end of the dock, I took off all my clothes and dove in.

I surfaced immediately. I couldn't breathe. It was so cold. Erin was on the dock laughing. I swam to the ladder to get out, and she stood above me looking at her watch. I pushed back away. Swimming backstroke as fast as I could. Anything to stay warm. Anything to win.

I stopped and shouted to her, "How much time left?"

"A minute and a half."

I couldn't believe I had been in the water for only thirty seconds. It was so hard to catch my breath. I started swimming freestyle. Pulling hard with my arms. Parallel to the shore. No reason to go out into the deeper water. The colder water. I began feeling numb. That was the best I could hope for. A lowering of the shock value.

"How much time now?" I yelled again while treading water.

"About a minute and twenty seconds more."

"No way. Check your watch again."

I knew she wasn't right, and when she began laughing I realized she was just having a little fun at my expense.

"OK, here's the truth," she said. "You've got about one minute to go."

I swam, and I swam, and I swam. And as I did I counted to sixty. When I reached the dock, I had her confirm my victory before getting out.

"You win," she said.

I climbed the ladder, and she wrapped me in the towel. I sat down on the warm dock. Shivering. Fingers and toes a hint of blue. She went to the car to get a sweatshirt and wool socks for me. I lay down to soak up more heat. When she returned, I put on the clothes she brought me and my shorts and boxers that had been lying in the sun. They felt so warm. Like just out of the dryer. My body started regaining the heat it had surrendered to the lake. Erin's arms around me.

We lay there in the sun all afternoon. Eventually Erin jumped in, but got out right away. A double-or-nothing bet she lost. We decided to stay there for the night. It was too late in the day to get back on the road. I walked around the white clapboard cottage checking doors and windows and found an unlocked first-floor window. No alarm. Nothing to steal from a summer cottage. Erin was nervous because they were friends of her family, and it would get back to her parents if we were caught. I thought that since Erin knew them that it wouldn't be a big deal if we were questioned by someone or even if the police did come. I climbed through the window and went to the back door and let Erin in. We walked around and checked the place out. The water had been turned on. Probably by a local caretaker. So we had use of the toilets, showers, and sink. Hot water too. Everything we needed for a night's stay.

There was a cool little restaurant in town. Right on the water. We sat at the bar. Oysters on the half shell. Labatt's on draft. Watched the sunset out the window. The lake losing its blues and greens and just slowly turning black like a bruise. When the door to the deck opened, I could feel the cool air. It reminded me of the water. There was a guitar player in the corner who didn't know any of the songs we wanted him to play. We became friends anyway.

We kept the lights off at the cottage. Even though we were hidden by the trees from the next closest cottage there was no need to draw attention, and there was no need for lights anyway. One of the bedrooms had a queen bed. Ours for the night. We kept our clothes on. Slept on top of the bed with my down sleeping bag unzipped over the top of us. It was plenty warm. And much easier than having to change sheets or make the bed in the morning. Nobody would ever know we were there. Without a trace. Like the wet outlines of our bodies on the dock that had dried in the sun. Our only footprint being the bottle of wine we picked up in town and left in the fridge as a small token of appreciation for the night's stay.

I claimed my prize in the morning, and then we took showers. Cleaned up the bathroom, straightened up the bed, and went out the unlocked window. Another beautiful day in the Northeast. We drove through the remaining

Finger Lakes. Then through Pennsylvania and Ohio. Not a cloud in the sky the whole day. Temperature in the mid-seventies. Traffic started backing up just outside of Cincinnati. Baseball time. People in their cars with their Reds hats on. It looked like fun. I talked Erin into going to the game. Hot dogs, beers, foul balls.

We bought a couple of cheap tickets in the nosebleeds and rooted the Reds on to victory against the Padres. At the seventh inning stretch we left. All the hotels in the area were full for the Friday night game, so we drove almost to Louisville, listening to the last couple of innings on the radio. We found a cheap but clean hotel, and sleep came instantly.

CHAPTER ELEVEN

At seven the next morning, an above-average-looking thirty-five-year-old woman with her dirty-blonde hair pulled back in a ponytail and out the back side of a John Deere baseball cap rang the doorbell of 17 Foot Hills Lane. Faded jeans, flip-flops, and a cream-colored V-neck T-shirt completed her attire. A brown suede purse was draped over her left shoulder.

Mark and Ellie Dempsey were in the kitchen having breakfast and reading the local news when they heard the chime. It was unusual to have someone at the door that time of day. They took their eyes off the print and glanced over at each other. A rock, scissors, paper look to see who was going to get up to see who it was. She won.

Mark walked to the door in his suit pants, shirt, and tie. His thinning light brown hair neatly parted to the side and his face freshly shaven. Wire-rimmed glasses in place. He looked out through the row of windows in the upper part of the door. Saw the woman. He then unlocked the deadbolt and opened the door.

"Good morning. What can I do for you?" he said in his usual business tone.

"Hello, sir. I was wondering if I could use your phone. My car broke down just around the corner, and I wanted to call a tow truck," she said, standing at attention with her hands behind her back.

He hesitated at first because it certainly was an odd situation. The time of day. The car not visible. But often hesitance gives way to politeness.

"Come on in," he said, swinging the door open for her. "We've got a phone in the kitchen."

He turned, and she followed him across the newly refinished hardwood floor. As they left the foyer and just prior to entering the hallway that led back to the kitchen, he was looking out the dining room window and saw a car pull into the driveway. He stopped. He turned to ask her if she knew who that was, but before he could get any words out she was holding a .38 pistol on him.

"Just keep moving to the kitchen," she said with pursed lips and squinted eyes. Looking tough as hell. He had never seen a woman look that way.

"Wait a second, what's going on here?" Mark asked in complete disbelief.

She heard the fear in his voice, and added to it by cocking the hammer of the gun.

"OK, lady, please. I'm doing what you want. Please don't point that gun at me."

"Don't say another word. Just keep moving."

When Ellie saw her husband and the gun trained on the back of his head, her hands began to quiver, still wrapped around her coffee cup. They were suddenly the only part of her body that could move, though not by her choosing. Still sitting at the kitchen table, she stared long and hard at the apparently crazy woman in their house coming toward her. Ellie's fear only escalated when she heard a car door shut and then a stranger appeared at her locked back door.

"Open the door," Kaylee instructed Ellie while she kept the gun pointed at her husband. Ellie didn't move. Still in shock. Trembling. Kaylee wasn't patient. She raised her voice and shouted, "Get the fuck up and open the door right now, or I'll blow your husband's head off."

Ellie pulled herself together and did as she was told. Lowell entered the kitchen brandishing his Smith & Wesson .357 Magnum. He shut the door and locked the deadbolt.

"Mr. and Mrs. Banker, take a seat," said Lowell, pulling out a chair at the kitchen table for Ellie. The same one she had been sitting on. The two of them sat down.

Coffee still warm. Sections of the paper strewn across the table where they had left them. Kaylee went around to the opposite side of Lowell in the kitchen. The Dempseys between them. "Let me start by informing you we're the type of people you don't want to get on the bad side of. And secondly, I don't like repeating myself. Understand?"

"Please, we don't want any trouble," Mark replied.

"Well, you won't get any trouble if you do exactly what we tell you to do and when to do it," Lowell told him. Mark nodded his head in submission. "We know you go to your bank every day at eight to open it up, but today you're going to get there a little early. Seven thirty, to be exact. And then you're going to round up thirty thousand dollars and walk out the back door and hand it to Mrs. Daniels here." He pointed to Kaylee with his gun.

"I want to be Mrs. Beam," Kaylee told him.

"I apologize," he said to Mark Dempsey. "You'll hand it to Mrs. Beam."

"We don't have thirty thousand dollars on hand like that. I can't get you that amount of money," said Mark.

"Don't insult me, Mr. Banker. Like I said before, we are not the type of people you want to irritate."

"I promise I'm not trying to insult you. I'm being honest," Mark replied. He knew the bank had $30,000, but it was his instinct to guard the bank. See if a lower number could be negotiated. He was a loyal officer of the employer.

"Is he telling the truth, Mrs. Banker?" Lowell asked her as he took a step toward her and put his left hand on her shoulder. The softness of her terry cloth robe. He squeezed it. The tight grip was alarming to Ellie. She wanted to stand up. Move away. But the grip was strong, and she knew better than to do anything but sit there. Grin and bear it. Anger welling up in Mark's face as he sat across the table watching this man with wild-looking eyes and a terrifying gun clamping down on his wife's shoulder with his paw.

"I don't know anything about the bank, but I'm certain my husband is telling the truth." Ellie's body was shaking. Lowell felt it in the grip of his hand.

Kaylee jumped in. "Your goddamn husband runs a bank, and you mean to tell us you know nothing about it?"

"Well then, I guess there's only one way to find out. Mr. Banker, Mrs. Beam here is going to follow you to the bank. I'm going to wait right here with your lovely wife. If Mrs. Beam doesn't arrive back here by eight fifteen with thirty thousand dollars, then I'm going to shoot your wife." He moved the .357 down to the front of Ellie's face. "Open your mouth, Mrs. Banker," Lowell demanded.

"Please leave my wife alone."

"Shut your goddamn mouth!" Kaylee shouted.

"Please don't make me do this," Ellie pleaded as her tears began flowing.

"I made it clear that I'm not in the habit of repeating myself. I'm not going to ask you again," Lowell said to her and squeezed her shoulder even harder. She opened up her mouth, shut her eyes, and Lowell slid the barrel in.

"We're eager to do business with you, Mr. Banker. Are you going to approve our credit and issue the loan?"

"Yes, yes, I can do it. Please take that out of her mouth. You're hurting her."

Lowell pulled the gun out of her mouth, looked at his watch, and then at Mark Dempsey. "I would advise you to get going. Time is money, Mr. Banker." He unlocked the deadbolt.

At seven thirty Mark Dempsey pulled into the bank parking lot. Kaylee trailing behind him and then parking at the rear of the bank by the door. Mark parked in his usual spot and then went to the front door and unlocked it. He went inside and turned off the alarm. He went over to the vault and entered the combination and opened it. The automatic timer expiring each morning at 7:00 a.m. He also opened up the cashiers' drawers. Within a few minutes he had counted up $30,000 and put it into two money bags. The security cameras inside the bank recording each action for posterity.

There was sweat on his forehead, and he wiped it as he unlocked the back door and stepped outside where Kaylee waited in the pickup. Windows down.

"Here's your money," Mark said, winded as he handed the bags to Kaylee through the window. "Now please just let my wife go. I've done what you've asked."

"There's been a slight change to our deal," Kaylee told him. The money, and the leverage he had with it, out of his hands and resting on the front seat.

"What do you mean?"

She pulled the gun up from her lap and aimed it at him through the opened window. There was no hesitation in Kaylee pulling the trigger. The .38 ripped open Mark Dempsey's stomach and he slumped back against the steel door. The recoil from the firearm knocked Kaylee's arm up into the top of the door frame where the metal was unforgiving. It smashed her thumb and she let go of the gun. It hit the bottom of the window frame on the door, and then fell to the pavement. Mark laboring to get air into his lungs, began leaning forward for the gun. Kaylee saw the look of hope in his eyes and thrust the car door into him. It slammed him back against the steel door of the bank, permanently. She got out of the car and picked up the gun.

"I don't think so," she said, and then fired the second round of Lowell's trademark one-two punch that went in and out of his brain.

CHAPTER TWELVE

S tanding on that trail, I couldn't move. Couldn't believe my eyes. The woman's arms were stretched out above her head in the shape of a church spire. They were tied together at the wrists with rope. Another piece of rope went from there to a tree branch above. She was almost suspended in air. Feet positioned to pirouette. Head hanging down. Body motionless. Wearing a ripped T-shirt that barely covered her chest. White underwear. A bloody wound top of her right foot. I was shocked.

Around her was a primitive-looking camp. A fire-pit ringed with stones. A tent and a lean-to made from pine and spruce branches, poles, and a big nylon tarp. Some trash lying about. A dirty-looking blue blanket spread out on the ground. There were two camouflage-print hunting-type backpacks leaning up against a tree. Tools next to it. An axe. I had no idea what I'd walked into. It put a chill deep inside me. A bizarre place.

Hearing my approach, she lifted her head. Her mouth was gagged and duct taped. She straightened up and saw me. We looked each other in the eye. I was forty feet away but felt like we were face-to-face. Her eyes grew wide, and I saw her trying to speak. She started twisting her body. Legs moving. Head turning back and forth with her dirty strawberry blonde hair bouncing around her shoulders.

It hit me. She was the missing woman from Wyoming that had been front-page news and all over AM radio. I could see her face just like in the magazine. Her pictures on TV. The runner. I couldn't believe it. It was her. Definitely her. I stopped, took a step toward her, and she began crying. Tears coming down her cheeks. Head nodding, indicating, "Yes, keep coming."

CHAPTER THIRTEEN

Day three on the road put us in the Midwest. A lot of farmland. The arch in Saint Louis. We jumped onto US 50 somewhere after Saint Louis and took that for a long stretch. I had remembered reading about it being the first transcontinental highway stretching from DC to San Francisco. We sped past small town after small town. Drank little Cokes in the thick glass bottles we'd get at gas stations. Wheat and cornfields as far as the eye could see. Every few miles I'd spy a hawk sitting on an old wooden fence post, waiting for its prey.

We got back on the interstate near Kansas City and made it to Hays, Kansas, by dusk. Grabbed a bite to eat and checked into the Holiday Inn.

"I'll call Carter and let him know we'll be there tomorrow night," I told Erin.

We were both really excited to be within striking distance of Aspen.

"OK, I'm going to go out and pick up cigarettes and a couple of things," she said. "Do you want beers or anything?"

"Beers sound good."

I called Carter at his house in LA. He didn't answer. Then I called the second number he had given me. He answered.

"Hey, Carter, its Alex and Erin."

"Hi, Alex. Good to hear from you guys. Are you on your way?"

He was talking loudly, and I could hear a busy restaurant in the background.

"Yeah, we're in Kansas, and should make it to your place early tomorrow night."

"Great. Make yourself at home. I'll have the key put in the mailbox for you."

"I really appreciate you helping us out like this."

"No problem," he replied.

"When are you and Kelley flying in?"

"Probably next weekend. Maybe even Thursday if I get the chance."

"Erin and I are really looking forward to seeing you guys, and let's make sure you and I get on the water." I wanted some way to return the favor by guiding him on the Roaring Fork.

"You got it."

I knew I'd caught him at a busy time and didn't want to keep him. The phone call was short and sweet, and it was good to know everything was working out as planned. It was a big help to have a place to stay for free while we looked for our new home.

Erin came back with beers, tampons, and a *People* magazine. Tabloid reading after the long day. We propped ourselves up on the bed and just hung out. The TV on. Neon lights glowing outside our window in Hays. Home of the Seventh Cavalry 120 years prior. Lieutenant Colonel George Armstrong Custer and his men. It had always fascinated me. Couldn't imagine being surrounded by thousands of pissed-off Indians and ammunition running low. The struggle to survive. There was a brochure about Fort Hays in the lobby, and I had put it on the nightstand. Something to read.

Erin was reading a story about a girl who disappeared in Laramie, Wyoming. It had made the national news and she'd been following it on the radio. A newlywed who jogged every day after work and then one night never returned. She was a pretty strawberry blonde, and they had a big article about the story in the magazine. Featured on the front-page. They were searching everywhere for her.

After a couple beers, I started to get a little tired. It was getting late. We had another long day of driving ahead. I got up and shut the curtain for the night. Turned off the TV and climbed into bed. Erin was still reading. Glued to the story. I shut my eyes and thought about my mom and dad. I missed them.

CHAPTER FOURTEEN

"This beautiful home and nice yard, but no children. I find that rather interesting," said Lowell, tapping his lips with the dirty nail of his index finger. "Care to elaborate?"

The question surprised her. She didn't know how to answer; the less they talked the better, she thought. Who knew how he would react to anything she said, so she chose to remain silent and tried avoiding eye contact. "It's a yes or no question, Mrs. Banker." Lowell stopped leaning back against the kitchen counter and stood up straight.

"No," she said.

"What's the matter, you and Mr. Banker aren't hitting it off in the bedroom?"

Ellie began getting even more nervous. She glanced at the clock on the wall and wished she could hear cars pulling into the driveway. Hoping her husband would be back any moment. That this nightmare would soon be over.

"We tried having children for years but were never able to conceive. Now you know." She looked away. Disgusted with having to explain it to this man whom she held in such contempt. A previous feeling of dread morphed into resentment.

"Maybe Mr. Banker's pockets run deep, but something else doesn't?" said Lowell as he took a step toward her, spun the chair around that Mark had been sitting in moments before, and sat down backward with the front of his torso against the back of the chair. Legs on either side of the seat like a saddle.

He reached over and felt her hair, and she pulled away. She thought about standing up. She thought about her ability to make it out the back door and running for the neighbors. He held the gun in his left hand, and it rested on the kitchen table. A foot from her hands. So close. There wasn't a chance, though, and she knew it. He was bigger and stronger.

He reached over for her hair again, and she slapped his hand. It was purely instinctual.

"I think you need to say you're sorry, Mrs. Banker."

She looked him in the eye. The proud woman she was. Emotions summiting.

"I'm not saying sorry to you. I want you out of my house. Now!"

The gun came off the table and slid into the back of his jeans. With both hands free, he grabbed her neck. In a spontaneous reaction her fingernails dug into his wrists. Blood was drawn. He let go and stood up. She fled for the door. He grabbed the back of her faded pink robe and kicked the door shut. Spun her around. Yanked the robe down off her shoulders. She tried to keep it on. A quick, strong tug and it lay on the white tile floor with her next to it. Fetal position in a white T-shirt and white lace underwear. He grabbed her by the hair and started dragging her out of the kitchen. She began crying.

"Please let go of me," Ellie pleaded as she slid across the tile floor.

"You had your chance to say you're sorry, Mrs. Banker. Too late now."

"Let go of me. You're hurting me."

The dining room had a hardwood floor and an area rug, and she stopped sliding when they reached that. While still holding her by the hair, he shoved the table aside and spread her out on the carpet. She immediately curled up. He straddled her just like he had done the kitchen chair, but now his knees were touching the floor. He grabbed her arms, spread them apart, and pinned her to the wool pile. A crucifixion without nails.

"Please don't do this," Ellie said, tears streaming down her face.

"What is it you think I'm going to do?" he asked as he let go of her arms and looked down at her, acting as though he was puzzled.

She took it as a sign of weakness and struck him in the face, hoping to knock him off of her and make it out the front door. But her blow only grazed him, and in retaliation he ferociously swung his arm across his body and swatted the side of her head with the back of his open right hand, which stunned her. He regained control of her arms and once again pinned them to the cross. They looked each other in the eyes. The dry and the watered.

Ellie gave up all forms of escape, except the one from reality. *This isn't happening* she told herself. *This is all just a bad dream. This isn't real.* Tears streamed down her face. Lowell watching her and feeling nothing.

The sound of a car pulling into the driveway brought Ellie back to the real world. Lowell got up and dragged her by the hair back into the kitchen. He unlocked the backdoor and Kaylee came inside.

"Did you get the money?" he asked.

"All of it. It's in the car,"

"Then let's get going."

He put the gun to Ellie's head. "Get up. We're going for a ride."

The pickup moved slowly over a dirt and gravel road that was littered with potholes. Ellie felt every one of them while handcuffed to a tie-down in the bed of the truck with the windowless truck cap sealed on top of her. Pitch-black world like the bottom of the sea. Sounds of the radio filtering in from the speakers in the cab. The heat was building. She had no idea where she was or where she was going. All she knew was that the end of her life was near. The things she wanted to say to her husband that she never said. A good-bye to her aging parents. She couldn't stop crying. Alone in her underwear and T-shirt. Feeling the bruises and soreness from Lowell's abuse.

The pickup came to a stop. She heard the driver's side door open and shut. A key inserted into the tailgate and then blue sky. Those eyes. Remote and remorseless. He reached in and unlocked the handcuffs, and then grabbed her by the armpits and pulled her out. He stood her up on the dirt road.

"Today's your lucky day, Mrs. Banker," Lowell said, and he walked back around, got into the cab, and wound his window back up to the halfway position. It would help with the dust they would soon be churning up again. He started the pickup and turned the vehicle around on the narrow road to head back out of the Wasatch National Forest. She stood there off to the side by the grove of aspen trees, and he stopped the vehicle next to her. Looked at her. "You've got a two-mile walk to the main road, where I'm sure you'll find someone to give you a lift home. I'd appreciate it if you took it nice and slow to give us plenty of time to be on our way without any trouble. Okay?"

"Okay," she replied.

"Nice meeting you, Mrs. Banker," Lowell said as he drove off.

She watched them drive away. When the dust settled, she began running. But the gravel was brutal on her bare feet. She had no choice but to walk, and with each step she prayed that her husband's fate was no worse than hers.

CHAPTER FIFTEEN

The Rockies began to appear on the horizon. Erin was driving, and I had her pull over so I could get a photo of them. I had never seen them from this far away before. During family trips, we had always flown into Denver. I loved how the prairie ended in such a dramatic fashion. I thought of the pioneers. Wagon trains full of families and their possessions. Seeing such an imposing natural wonder blocking their way west, and meeting the challenge head on.

There was no stopping in Denver. Climbed up I-70 and through the amazing Eisenhower Tunnel. Down into Dillon. Memories of family ski trips to Keystone. Then back up to the Vail Pass. A roller coaster of highway travel. Runaway truck ramps. We stopped in Vail for gas and a bag of Fritos. We followed the Colorado River through the majestic Glenwood Canyon and popped out at Glenwood Springs. We were an hour away from Aspen. We turned onto Highway 82 and saw Mount Sopris through the windshield. Kept it in our sights as we continued on to Carbondale and Basalt, the confluence of the Roaring Fork and Frying Pan Rivers. Then Woody Creek where the rock stars and movie stars lived.

We drove past the Maroon Bells around dinnertime, and that's when we were officially new residents of Aspen. Erin leaned over and gave me a kiss on my cheek. It was a beautiful early-June night. I pulled over to the side of the road to look at the directions to Carter's place. We were close. A few minutes away.

The key was in the mailbox. It was a good feeling when I saw it. We unloaded our things onto the front steps. I carried the heavy stuff. Erin went inside to check out the house. I kept unloading.

She came back out.

"There's a first-floor bedroom that we should use," she said. "It's a really cool place. You're going to love what's out back."

She propped open the front door, and the two of us started carrying everything to our room. Looking through a big sliding glass door to the backyard, I saw the Roaring

Fork River. A hundred feet away! Couldn't wait to fish it. Be in that water. It felt like a fantastic dream to actually be there. With Erin.

It took us two full days of apartment shopping to find our own place: a modest one-bedroom apartment. Immediate occupancy and within walking distance to town. Month-to-month lease. Affordable, in terms of Aspen pricing. And its fireplace sealed the deal.

We were lucky to find the new apartment. It wouldn't be long before the town began filling up again with its seasonal ebb and flow of people. High tide in summer and winter. The resort town swelled in ranks when the mountains can be skied, and when they can be hiked in shorts. It was also admired as the backdrop of music and arts festivals. And their renowned streams filled with rising trout during mayfly hatches.

A free ski pass was the only major requirement for my job search. As I found out it was a benefit certain employers offered, those were the ones I sought out. I knew that all employees of the Aspen Ski Company received one, but I didn't want to be a lift operator or clean condos. Not a good fit. And I couldn't wait until the ski season opened to start work. I needed a source of income right away.

My experience in climbing, fishing, hiking, and skiing enabled me to get hired at Aspen Mountain Sports. They sold outdoor gear, products I knew and used. It was a retail job mostly, with a standard hourly wage. But I liked the guys who worked there, got 50 percent off on everything in the store, and it came with a ski pass after three months of employment. I happily signed on.

Erin checked in with the art galleries in town, and in the process met a new friend, Megan Singleton. The two of them hit it off right away. Mostly staffed by the owners and their friends, none of the galleries were hiring. One of the owners liked her, though, and gave her a name at Obermeyer, a brand name in ski wear based in Aspen. They were hiring. Erin's two years in fashion and her BA in studio art might give her a shot at a position there.

She had three interviews over two days, and then they offered her a job in their design department. It was a great job for her. A real job. She jumped in my arms and told me the good news. Called her mom and dad. They talked for an hour. She told them all about our new place, about Megan, all the great people she'd met at Obermeyer, how she was going to work really hard, how much she liked the town, how she couldn't wait for them to come visit. She was so happy. Within a week of our arrival in mid-June, we had found a new home and jobs. It was all working out.

CHAPTER SIXTEEN

It was a frightening scene, and somehow I had stumbled into the middle of it. For a second I thought about just getting out of there. Maybe my life was in danger. *Run.* This wasn't a good place. Avoid trouble at all costs. I was carrying forty pounds of uncut cocaine. I had to get to the lake. All this flashed through my frenzied mind.

I took off my backpack and laid it on the trail. Unzipped the side pocket and pulled out my knife. Stood up and took another look around. There was no one around but me and her. I could see the tent and lean-to were empty. Quickly I went over to her. Holding my hands up to let her know I was there to help while saying the same in a low voice. The knife frightened her. I lowered it and then remembered her name.

"Are you Sarah?" I asked. She nodded yes. She tried saying it. "I'm going to cut you down. Everything is going to be alright."

Raising the knife high, I cut the rope suspending her. She dropped, collapsing on the ground before I could catch her. Her wrists were still tied. I cut that rope as well. She removed the duct tape and took out the gag. I lifted her up. She wrapped her arms around me and began crying.

"Please get me out of here," she said. "They're here somewhere." Tears poured down her face.

I could see the sheer terror in her eyes.

"Who's here, Sarah?"

"I want to go home," she said, trembling. "Please get me out of here. Please, please."

"Tell me who they are and where they are."

"There are two of them. They're crazy. They come and go. I think they went down to the river. They have guns. We have to leave now!" She was shaking, and I held on to her with both of my hands just above her biceps. I had never seen anyone so frightened, and her fear was contagious. I wanted out of there too.

"Follow me," I told her.

CHAPTER SEVENTEEN

M y life changed forever when I picked up Carter at
Sardy Field, the airport in Aspen. It was a small
favor he had asked of me. The guy who usually picked
him up wasn't available. It was a Saturday, and I was off
work. Glad to help him out. He insisted I use his car. Erin
dropped me off at his house, and I picked up his Blazer
and drove it to the airport.

Waiting for him, I looked up in the sky for a Beech
King Air. It was his new toy, or new to him: a two-year-old
plane built in 1983. He told me all about it on the phone.
It was the F90. Twin turboprop. Four-bladed propellers;
270-knot cruising speed. Range of 1778 nautical miles. LA
to Aspen in a few hours. Carter loved flying and could talk
about it all day.

He was right on time. Eleven thirty. He came out of the clouds toward me and banked hard left to line up for a landing into the wind. The chrome of the propeller cones glittering intermittently in the partly sunny sky. When it touched down and sped past me, I read the call letters on the tail, confirming it was his plane.

I got in his car and drove to meet him. He parked in a row of jets and turboprops, swinging it into position. Engines still running. Blades still turning. I kept my distance. I could see him in the cockpit with his headphones on. Kelley wasn't with him. Just himself. He shut the engines off, and everything became quiet. OK to approach. I parked his car right in front of his plane and got out and waved to him. He waved back and took off his headphones. Ray-Ban Aviator sunglasses still on.

The side door on the plane opened up, and out he came in jeans and a navy-blue Izod polo shirt.

"Welcome to Aspen, Carter."

We shook hands.

"Good to see you, Alex, and thanks for picking me up."

"It's the least I could do. How was your flight?"

"Very smooth. This plane really flies well."

I peeked inside the plane to check it out. Very nice. Beautiful wood trim and leather seats. He opened the cargo door and then asked me to give him a hand. He had a couple of duffel bags and a suitcase. We loaded them into his Blazer. A service attendant pulled up in a golf cart, and Carter talked to him. Told him he'd be there for a few days and would need the plane refueled.

After helping him secure the plane, we left the airport and headed back to his place. He was driving.

"I thought Kelley was coming with you," I said, knowing that Erin was going to be disappointed. He pulled the cigarette out of his mouth and looked over at me.

"We got into a fight last night, and she's all mad at me. She thinks I'm too close to this girl who works at one of my restaurants. It's all in her head." He looked sincere. "I keep telling her that I'm always going to be around other girls. I'm in the restaurant business." He flicked his cigarette out the window. "So how are things with you?"

"Everything is great, and I want to thank you again for letting us stay at your place last week. It really helped us out."

"Anytime. Is Erin liking it out here?"

"She does. She got a great job at Obermeyer."

"I thought that's what Kelley told me. How about you?"

"I'm working over at Aspen Mountain Sports. It's limited hours right now until the season picks up, but I think it's going to work out. If you need anything just let me know, and I can get you fifty percent off."

We pulled up to the stoplight by the Hotel Jerome. He grabbed another cigarette and lit it with the car lighter. I could tell something was on his mind.

"Can you keep something between us?" he asked me.
"Sure."

I was looking at him, and he looked at me. The light turned green, and he began driving. He took a left on Galena. Came to a stop by this manicured field that I wasn't familiar with. It was an odd question. Maybe he did cheat on Kelley after all. Maybe she caught him and that's why he'd arrived solo.

"Let's get out and talk over here," he said, and we got out and walked over to the little park.

We stood a few feet away from the hood of his Blazer. In the shade of a pine tree. No one around.

"How would you like to make some money?" he said.

Point-blank. Everything changed in an instant from casual to business. I didn't move to Aspen to make money. I was there to play before heading into the real world and getting a real job making money. But I was intrigued, and the element of the unknown was exciting. For some reason I liked feeling those butterflies in my stomach, and I knew by the way he looked at me that he wasn't going to ask me to start some new restaurant with him. It was something under the table. That's why we were talking where we were.

"What do you mean?" I could tell he knew I was guarded, but still curious.

"I haven't known you all that long, Alex, but I think I'm a pretty good judge of people. I think I can trust you." I looked him in the eye and nodded yes. He continued. "In one of the duffel bags in the back of my car is forty pounds of coke." I wasn't as surprised as I possibly could've been. It didn't shock me. The plane. The restaurants. The blow he gave me the first night we met. It all added up quickly. He took one last drag of his half-smoked cigarette, dropped it to the ground, and stepped on it. Turning his foot back and forth. "The less I tell you, and the less you ask, the better off you are," he said.

"OK," I replied as I began looking for the exit sign.

"I need someone to put it in a backpack and hike it in to Oar Lake on the other side of the pass, exchange it for cash, and then hike back out. It's an overnight trip. I'll pay you ten grand."

Time to go. Run, don't walk. Run fast! I knew what the right thing was to do. This was nothing but trouble, and the best course of action was to walk away from it. Sprint, if I had to. It was so obvious. But what completely caught me off guard—as much as his proposal—was how quickly I was able to look far down the road and project an image of me and Erin arriving there. I saw LA and New York, either of which I had agreed to move to after Colorado, and knew the cost of living in those cities was three times that of Aspen where we were living from paycheck to paycheck—as planned—without concern for rainy days or nest eggs. The future, though, was eventually going to catch up with us, and when it did, the money would keep us from having to climb out of a hole. Ten grand was a huge amount. I was making six bucks an hour at the store. I'm sure Carter could see the temptation in my eyes. And so I actually began feeling lucky to be having the conversation with him. An opportunity had fallen into my lap, and the longer I held it there, the louder it knocked.

"Do you know the area?" he asked.

"Not all that well. I've camped before out by Windsor Lake, and I've fished Cameron Creek, which I think is somewhere over in that area. It's been a few years though. Tell me more."

"There's an old mining trail that's just outside of town here that goes all the way to the most southern point of Nast Tunnel Diversion Road on the other side of the pass, and a few hundred yards beyond that is Oar Lake. It's about a thirteen-mile hike in. I've got maps and can show you everything."

"And what do I do when I get there, if I were to do this?" I asked.

"There'll be a guy waiting there for you. It's a small, remote lake, and he'll almost definitely be the only person there. He'll just be there fishing. Waiting for you. He'll be wearing an Atlanta Braves baseball hat, and he'll have a backpack too. You'll switch loads. Money for the coke."

"How much money?"

"It's the amount I charge for flying it in on my plane from LA. You won't need to count it. It will be wrapped up in plastic just like the coke," he said. I didn't say a thing. He paused and could tell I wanted to know what his cut of the deal was. "It's two hundred thousand dollars, which is ten percent of the value of the coke. Airplanes and pilots don't come cheap."

I wanted to say, "But guys like me do," but I realized quickly that I was the low man on the totem pole, and that's how it goes in the business world. I was learning. "So you've obviously done this before," I said.

He looked around again to see if we were still alone. I did the same. We both moved a little more into the shade.

"Let me fill you in a little because I can see all the questions in your eyes. And it's cool. I totally understand. I would be the same," he began. I had lots of questions, but it was time to just listen. "A few years ago I met some people who wanted to invest in my restaurant business. They were friends of friends of friends. It didn't take me long to figure where their money came from. They had lots of it, and they wanted to launder it through my restaurants. Make it cleaner. I even had the option of buying restaurants or franchises using their money and retaining a majority interest." I was following along. He looked around again before continuing on with the history lesson. "I gave it some thought, but in the end I wasn't interested in taking on partners with ties across the border. I just thought things could get messy, and there would be too many things out of my control. Besides, I was doing well enough on my own."

"So you walked away?"

"Almost." He went over and reached inside his four-wheel drive and grabbed the pack of cigarettes on the dashboard. A chain smoker. Took one out and lit it with his lighter. "A few weeks later they offered me a slightly different deal. They knew I was a pilot, and maybe that's what they wanted me for all along. They offered me a bunch of cash to fly coke into the Denver area. That changed the picture for me because I would just be operating as a courier. Like FedEx. I had a Cessna 310, and there's nothing more I like to do than fly. Well, almost nothing," he said with a sly smile.

"Why Denver?" I asked, keeping it all business and not getting sidetracked with his sexual reference.

"It's one of the fastest-growing cities. I guess they have a network there to distribute it throughout the city and all across the Rockies. Some of it probably comes right back up here to Aspen."

"Business 101," I said.

"It's no different than the way McDonald's thinks," he said, exhaling smoke.

"But what about the risk?"

"No doubt there's a lot of risk, and I definitely don't want to lose my freedom. People who make mistakes get caught. They get greedy and careless. I only make five or six flights a year for them. Call it a hobby."

I believed what he was telling me as the two of us stood there. A guy I really didn't know but who had been nothing but generous to me. I wondered what Kelley knew about him. My gut kept telling me to walk away. Just move on and say, "No thanks." But that element of the unknown, the adventure, and the easy money I could make for just hiking the mountains that I loved being up in was difficult to say no to. Too difficult. Standing there, I began to feel my first foot entering the water. I wanted to hear more details. Then it would be easier to put the second one in.

"So why do you need someone to hike it in to the lake? Why not just drive it there?"

"It's safer that way," he replied.

"What do you mean?"

"I used to fly it directly into Denver. There's a small general aviation airport there for planes like mine and some of the corporate jets in the area. It was easy. But after a couple of summers I thought it was time to change things. Again, trying to stay ahead of the game. If you get complacent you start making mistakes, and that leads to trouble."

"Sounds like the smart thing to do," I told him, stoking his ego a bit.

"So I came up with the idea of flying into Aspen. I bought a place here, which gives me a legitimate reason for coming back and forth. It looks more normal than my trips to Denver. And real estate prices just keep going up here. A good investment as well, and I'm going to learn how to catch more fish than you," he said, flashing that charming smile of his.

I smiled too. His comment about fishing sort of broke the ice. Made me more comfortable. Relaxed.

"I'll be happy to teach you what I know, as long as I get a lifetime membership to the Roaring Fork behind your house," I said.

"You got it."

We both seemed much more at ease with each other. I wasn't thinking about consequences anymore. In a strange way, I felt lucky to have met him. I then asked him to tell me more about the hike to the lake. I wanted to hear the rest.

He went on.

"For my first couple of flights into Aspen, they had someone drive up from Denver to pick up the coke. It all went well. But the more I thought about it the more I realized that it was just too simple of a plan. We didn't take enough precautions. The guy even drove up to my plane, and we loaded it into his trunk and went our separate ways. It didn't take a lot of time, but what if someone was watching? Maybe I'm too paranoid?"

"Better safe than sorry."

"Well, that's how I feel too. You have to stay ahead of the game. I had to change things."

A car drove by us. Slowly. I could see it out of the corner of my eye. Carter stopped talking and turned his head. The car stopped. The reverse lights lit up, and it came back toward us. It made me a little nervous. It turned out to be two girls in their late teens, and the one in the passenger seat with the low-cut T-shirt full of breasts asked us if we knew how to get to North Spring Street. Carter directed them.

"Got to love Aspen," he said as they drove off.

It was hard to deny. Had lost my virginity during my junior year in high school when my parents rented a place in Aspen for July and August. She was a local. Pretty. Grew up quick. I could imagine her in that car.

When they turned the corner and went out of sight, he turned back to me.

"The airport was not a good place, and I came up with the idea of meeting somewhere much more remote. A place that would be hard to be followed to, photographed, or anything like that." He took a puff of his cigarette and continued. "There have been a few busts in the mountains recently, and a few in Denver," he said, looking at me in the eyes. I knew he could tell that put some fear into me. "I won't sugarcoat it for you. People get caught. But that's why I think you can never go too far with being careful. If a thirteen-mile hike to a remote lake greatly reduces the odds of getting busted, robbed, or screwed over, then I'm willing to pay a little more for the insurance."

I nodded in agreement and kept listening.

"Highway 82 is the only way in and out of Aspen, and I want to avoid the Pitkin County Sheriff's patrols on it and the highway patrol too. They're getting pressure to make busts. They're down in Glenwood Springs looking for people coming and going from I-70, and they're up by Independence Pass checking out that end of things. Using cars to transport it on Highway 82 is playing with fire. They're randomly pulling people over using some lame excuse just to check them out. Anything that might be odd. If they find something, they do a full search. And the popularity of *Miami Vice* hasn't helped things. They all think they're Crockett and Tubbs now."

He explained things pretty well. It added up. I didn't like hearing about people getting caught and the stepped-up efforts of the sheriff's office, DEA, highway patrol, or whoever, but I liked how he took precautions and almost went too far to avoid trouble. Better than the other way. I was in.

"Have you hiked the trail?" I asked.

"I haven't, and I really don't think I'm in good enough shape to do it. I'm just the pilot," he said somewhat sarcastically. "It's been done before though, if that's what you mean."

"Yeah, that's kind of what I was getting at."

"We did it about a month ago. I learned about the trail from a guy I got to know out here. He told me about it, and he was willing to do it. It all went well. There were no problems." He looked at me and knew my next question before I even said it. "But he moved to Oregon. I have the maps, though, and the same backpack he used, and some other things that might be useful to you."

"How about twelve grand and I'll do it," I said. Just like that the words came out.

He looked away for a second as I wondered what he'd paid the last guy. Was I being greedy, or was I leaving money on the table? I went high like my professors taught me.

He reached out and put his arm on my shoulder. "I'll give you fourteen grand if you can do it tomorrow. The weather forecast is great for the next few days."

I said yes, and I would've said yes to the ten grand if he had held firm, even though he had made it obvious he was anxious to get the coke out of his own hands and into someone else's. I was sold.

We got back into his Blazer and went back to his place. On the way we talked about the importance of keeping this to ourselves. Not even Kelley or Erin could know. I would lie, telling Erin that I was hiking in to do some fishing, that I got a report that the conditions were ideal. Hatches were taking place. Fish were rising. It wouldn't be that unusual. An overnight trip to a trout stream. She'd believe me. I'd get someone at work to cover my shifts. It was slow there right now and wouldn't be a problem. People were looking to pick up hours.

At his place we went over the maps and details. First thing in the morning he would drive me to the end of this dirt road not too far from his place where the trail named Mineral King began. The coke would be all wrapped up and waterproofed in the backpack. Sleeping bag, water purifier, compass, fly rod, flies, fishing license, clothes, and my other camping gear packed as well. The guy at the lake would be wearing an Atlanta Braves baseball hat. I'd give him the coke, he'd give me the money. Twenties and tens. It would be lighter than the coke. I hoped. It would be wrapped up and waterproofed just like the merchandise. Make a quick exchange and head home on the trail. Carter would be waiting for me where he dropped me off.

CHAPTER EIGHTEEN

As he waited for Ellie Dempsey to come trotting down the road—longer than Lowell normally would've because of the gravel that impeded her travels—he saw a plume of dust from an oncoming car. He hurried back to his pickup that was parked on the side of the road with Kaylee waiting in the front seat. He hadn't planned on encountering another vehicle on that remote stretch of the Wasatch, and he was even more surprised to see it was a park ranger.

The sedan approached slowly, and when it pulled up alongside, the ranger rolled down his window to see if the visitors in the pickup needed assistance. It was unusual for a vehicle to be parked on that narrow stretch of dirt and gravel just beyond a sharp bend that left them vulnerable to being rear-ended or side-swiped. Unusual, but nothing more than that.

"Anything I can help you with?" the ranger asked.

Lowell had rolled his window down when he saw the ranger doing the same. His cocked .357 below the window opening and hidden from the ranger's line of sight. As the ranger waited for the motorist to respond, Lowell drew his weapon and fired two shots in quick succession. The ranger never had a chance. The bullets struck in the head and neck, killing him instantly.

Lowell put on his gloves, got out of the pickup and into the ranger's car. He pushed the body to the other side of the front seat. "Wait for me here. I'll be back soon," he said to Kaylee as he put the ranger's hat on his head and drove off.

He went looking for Ellie disguised as the ranger. He followed the road back to where he had dropped her off but saw no sign of her along the way. He assumed that the shots he fired had startled his prey and sent her scampering into the woods for cover. As tempting as it was for him to hunt her down, he knew her husband's body would soon be discovered and the police would be on high alert and the roads would be heavily patrolled. He turned on the loudspeaker and picked up the mic. "Mrs. Dempsey, this is Ranger—," he paused—too long to be convincing—to look at the dead man's name tag, "Edmonds. Everything's okay. Your assailant has been shot and killed. It's okay to come out. You're safe." He waited and looked all around for her but there was no movement or any type of disturbance in the undergrowth. He tried one more time to call her in. A moment later he looked at his watch and realized he had no choice but to turn around and make an exit from the state of Utah as soon as possible.

He drove back to Kaylee and found a space large enough between the pines and aspens to drive the ranger's sedan off the road and into the forest where it was out of view. After he threw some decaying brush over it, he got in the pickup and the two of them made their escape.

In Rock Springs, Wyoming they purchased a used van and then burned their pickup beyond recognition in Diamondville. They kept moving from town to town, altering their appearances: Kaylee dyeing her hair black, Lowell cutting his short and starting to grow a beard. They stayed at campgrounds and motels. Kaylee paying cash and registering as the guest, with Lowell slipping in after dark—doing everything possible to avoid being seen together in public.

Every branch of law enforcement in the Mountain West was now hunting them, the infamous couple they'd become.

Crystal McCullough, a friend of Kaylee's since childhood, had a small place in a run-down section of Laramie. Two weeks of being on the run, they made their way there. Crystal put the two of them up. She knew they were on the run, but that was all she knew. They gave her two grand for the accommodations, and for not asking too many questions.

CHAPTER NINETEEN

Kerrigan was asleep when the phone on the nightstand rang at midnight. He picked it up before the second ring in his attempt to keep his wife from being awakened, but it had stirred her.

"Rory, it's Russ," said Lamar. "Sorry to wake you. We got our break, and it's a big one."

The FBI agent sat up in bed in the darkness. "I'm all ears."

"Turns out our 'boys' aren't. They're Bonnie and Clyde."

"Really, what have you got?"

"I was just on the phone with Gayle and she said our friends were up in Ogden, Utah where they invaded the home of a bank manager and held his wife hostage while he went to the bank to get their thirty thousand dollar ransom. After he gave Bonnie the money, she shot him. A bank employee found him dead by the rear entrance."

"These are some sick fucks, Russ."

"There's more," said Lamar. Kerrigan switched the phone to his other ear and rubbed his hand through his hair in anguish. "They take the money and the guy's wife and drive her to a remote area in the Wasatch National Forest. My details get a little sketchy from here, but apparently they let her go and somehow come across a park ranger that they shoot point blank while he's sitting in his car. Ballistics confirmed it's the same .357."

"When we find them, I'm going to take their .357 and shoot them with it. I kid you not."

"I'm with you," said Lamar.

"Tell me the banker's wife is okay."

"From what I've been told, she is. They roughed her up, but she's been released from the hospital. I told Feldman in Salt Lake that we'd fly up there first thing in the morning, and then drive from there to Ogden."

"Why don't we leave now?"

"It wouldn't do us any good. The woman's sedated and staying with relatives. Besides, she's had enough for one day."

"Okay. But I'm still heading in to the office. You coming in?"

"I'm here now."

CHAPTER TWENTY

Sarah Porter met Paul Evans in Laramie, Wyoming, in 1983. She had been transferred there for her job with ConAgra. Part of a research team working in conjunction with the University of Wyoming on ways to grow things quickly. Much quicker than Mother Nature herself. She was a biologist. A fresh Stanford grad with all the credentials, and her good looks didn't hurt. She had the unique combination of tanned skin and strawberry blonde hair. Green eyes. Fit and trim body on a five-foot-four-inch frame.

The area of agricultural science appealed to her. ConAgra was a good fit. Her family had been in the agriculture business for sixty years. Big landowners and produce businesses in Sacramento, California. It was in her blood to make things sprout from the soil, or a petri dish. Find out how it all works. How to improve upon it.

She liked her job and worked long hours. Being new to the area, she had yet to establish a social life. That was the hard part. A big change from Palo Alto. They had told her she would be there two years. Possibly longer. She could handle that. It was a good company that paid well and kept their promises to their employees. At least to the ones she spoke to prior to accepting the job. If she excelled, eventually she could write her own ticket. Potentially transfer to corporate or a major market research center. Move up into management. Head her own team. They would continue to invest in her and make her that much more valuable to the company. If things didn't work out, she had the family businesses to fall back on. But first she would try to make it on her own.

Every day after work she ran. Five miles. Sometimes more. Right out her door and onto the roads and sidewalks of her neighborhood. The farther she ventured the fewer cars there were. Open air. Tunes on her Sony Walkman. Hitting stride.

On a fall Saturday morning she decided to try a new route near the university. There was a park there that she wanted to run through. She heard it was pretty. A neighborhood of older homes surrounded it, as well as some city landmarks. Sarah would check it all out at seven miles per hour.

In the middle of her run, in the park's center, she spotted an old drinking fountain. Time for a break. It was Saturday morning. No hurry. The water would replenish what the few beers with her coworkers the night before had taken away. She stepped on the pedal. Nothing. Tried it again. Still no water shooting up through the spout. She gripped the underside of the bowl for leverage and this time pushed down as hard as she could on the pedal.

With her Walkman on, she did not hear the guy coming up behind her. He tapped her on the shoulder and startled her. He introduced himself. Paul was a runner too. He lived in the area. Knew the old drinking fountain needed a heavier man's weight to get it flowing. He stepped on the pedal and held it down while she drank.

He was a handsome guy in the insurance business, a few years older than her, and his timing couldn't have been better. For both of them. They started dating, fell in love, and within a year and a half got married. They bought a house with a great view of the Snowy Range Mountains, made lots of friends, and became firmly entrenched in the Laramie community. Charities, work, and her pursuit of her master's kept them happily busily.

By June of 1985, Sarah was regularly doing eight-mile runs after work. The New York Marathon was in her sights. She'd always wanted to do it. Maybe Paul would join her, but he hadn't been running as much lately.

On a Tuesday, Sarah made it home by six thirty. Paul wasn't there. She didn't know where he was. She changed into her running shorts and a T-shirt, and out the door she went. Leaving a note for Paul on the kitchen counter to let him know she'd gone running. With her Walkman on, she waved to Laura Gioberti at the end of her street before turning right onto North Fifteenth Street.

Paul worked late at his office that day. As the owner of a small business that he was determined to grow, he often did. His three employees had left at five o'clock. The weather was beautiful, and they wanted to enjoy it. He made it home by eight thirty. He was tired. Sarah wasn't home. He read her note and heated up the leftover Chinese takeout in the microwave. He ate it on their back deck, expecting Sarah's return any minute.

By the time he finished his meal, the sun was going down behind the mountains. He went into their bedroom and looked for Sarah's running shoes. Maybe she had come home and gone back out, forgetting to throw away the note. Maybe she was down the street at Laura's. The shoes weren't there. He called Laura. She told him she saw Sarah heading out for her run around six thirty. Eight miles usually only took her a little over an hour.

Something was wrong. He made more calls. None of their friends had seen or heard from her. He got in his car and went looking. An hour later, Paul pulled back into his driveway. He went inside and called the Laramie Police Department. It was 10:27 p.m.

The next morning every news vehicle around was camped out in front of Sarah and Paul's house. The story had broken. A massive search for Sarah was under way. Hundreds of people were involved. Police, friends, random volunteers. Groups on horseback, special dogs, helicopters. Nothing was found. Not a trace of her. More detectives were brought in. And then the Feds got involved. Sarah and Paul's families flew in. The whole thing got bigger and bigger. By the fifth day, it made the national news. People were talking about it everywhere.

CHAPTER TWENTY-ONE

They felt the noose tightening in Laramie and realized that no city or town was safe. Wherever there were people they'd be vulnerable to being identified and captured. Lowell came to the conclusion their only choice was to head into the backcountry of the mountains until things quieted down. Growing up in Carbondale, Colorado—thirty miles down river of Aspen—he spent much of his young-adult life hunting in the White River National Forest and knew just the place to go that was isolated and remote where they wouldn't cross paths with anyone. A place where there was an old abandoned forest service shelter that was once used as a fire prevention lookout, but had long since been abandoned after an avalanche caused it to go into disrepair. He had used the dilapidated structure many times, but it had been years since he'd been there and wasn't certain if it would still be standing. If not, they would have their tent, and poles and a tarp for a lean-to.

Lowell had seen her running on the side of the empty road each of the three trips he made to the dry-goods store to pick up supplies needed for their existence in the wild. The store was initially chosen because of its remote location on the outskirts of town where there was little traffic on the roads and in the aisles, but after laying eyes on her during his first venture into that section of Laramie, she was the driving factor for each of his subsequent trips. She captivated him with her strawberry-blonde hair and a body that was slender and muscular, each of her strides revealing the vitality of her youth. A college girl— his overriding fantasy during his years in prison— from the university, he surmised, far away from campus where street smarts—which he presumed she possessed little of or none at all—played to his advantage, not hers.

After his last trip to the store, he returned to Crystal's in the early evening and was sitting alone with Kaylee on the rotting back deck. A clumsily made wooden table and two chairs for them to sit on.

"How much do you love me?" he asked.

"Why do you always ask me that question?"

"Because I like the answer you give me."

"Okay, I love you like the stars."

"What if you were the stars and I wanted the moon as well?"

"Then I'd give you that too," she told him. "We've gone over this before. Many times."

"No questions asked?"

"No questions asked."

He could see that she had one though and was fairly certain what it was. "Go ahead and ask. I'll give you one," he said.

"You finally found her, right?"

"I did."

Kaylee looked beyond him toward the foothills. After gathering her thoughts she turned back to him and said, "If she's the girl of your dreams, then what am I?"

"The woman in them."

Two days later, Lowell and Kaylee saw Sarah running in the distance ahead. Technically with traffic, but there was none, just as it had been for Lowell the previous times. The two-lane road was straight and they had a clear view of it in both directions through the windshield and the mirrors, the sun to the west of them in full cooperation. At fifty-five miles per hour, they quickly gained on her.

"Drop it down to forty five," Lowell told Kaylee when they were within two-hundred yards of her. She eased off the accelerator. Lowell kept checking his side mirror that he had positioned to see the road behind him. It remained clear. He glanced at the speedometer. "Lower it to thirty." She tapped the brakes. He checked the mirror one more time. "Twenty, fifteen. Keep it there." When the front bumper of the van paralleled the runner, Lowell opened his door and slammed it into her back.

It thrust Sarah to the pavement and knocked the wind out of her.

"Hit the brakes," Lowell instructed Kaylee. The van came to a halt. He jumped out of the vehicle and swooped down on her. The eagle and the trout. He picked her up, along with the broken Sony Walkman and earphones and shoved her into the van through the side door. "Go, go, go," he fired off, and Kaylee sped the van away.

Gasping for air, Sarah's wrists were handcuffed to the floor ties in the cargo area of the van heading south for Colorado. When she was able to get air back into her lungs, the pain from the door slamming into her back set in.

In less than fifteen seconds, Sarah Evans had disappeared from the world.

CHAPTER TWENTY-TWO

S he fled with me as best she could. It hurt her to put weight on her right foot. The wound did not look good. She held on to my shirt with a tight grip. We got to my backpack, and I strapped it on, at the same time looking all around. We left the way I came, though much more swiftly. I could feel her grip on my backpack. Pulling her along.

She began to wince with every other step. Her bare feet on the gravel and sticks. The wound. I stopped.

"Are your shoes back there?" I asked her.

"I think they're by the tent."

"I have to go back and get them." I knew we wouldn't be able to make it far without her shoes, and I was upset with myself for leaving without them.

"You can't leave me here," she said, and she reached and grabbed hold of the front of my shirt.

"You'll be OK. I'll be right back."

"No, no, don't—" she pleaded.

"Listen, we have a long way to go, and you'll never make it without your shoes. Just stay here," I said firmly.

She sat down. Hidden in the shrubs, trees, and boulders. I took off my backpack and headed back. Heart racing. I stayed low and moved quickly. It didn't take long to reach the lip in the trail where I could see the camp. Flat on my stomach. I checked it out. Empty. I got up and raced to the tent. Her running shoes were on the far side of it next to her shorts. I grabbed both.

As I turned to leave the tent, I heard people coming up from the back side of the camp. Voices. I took off running as fast as I could. I didn't look back. Just kept running. They would be coming for us as soon as they saw the cut rope, so we needed as much distance between us and them as we could get.

I was sweating hard when I reached her.

"Quick, put these on," I said, handing her the shoes and shorts. Sweat and fear all over my face.

"What's wrong?" she asked.

"I heard them. We've got to go."

She started shaking again. The thought of them terrified her.

It was clearly painful for her to put on her right shoe. Her wound was bleeding, but she got them on. I tied one while she tied the other. She took the shorts with the

ConAgra logo on them and stood up and put them on. At the same time I strapped on my backpack, and we got moving.

We traveled as fast as we could, a pace somewhere between a fast walk and a slow jog. Her injured foot handicapped her as much as the weight of my backpack did me. We circled around the small lake or pond.

Fatigued, she tugged on my pack just as we reached the boulder which I now realized bore her name. I bent over to catch my breath too and pointed to her scratches on the rock. Both of us seemingly too winded to speak. With a nod, she acknowledged her markings. That riddle was solved, or so I thought.

"I have to stop," she panted, and then right away she turned and appeared to vomit. But nothing came out. She was sick. Her body bent over with her hands on her knees. Again another dry heave. Same result.

I straightened back up and watched her. I didn't know what to do.

"What's your name?" she asked.

"I'm Alex."

"Thank you, Alex," she said, hands still on her knees.

"You're going to be alright, but we have to keep moving."

"I'm sorry," she replied, beginning to cry.

But then she composed herself. I didn't have to say a thing. She straightened up, and off we went. We had to put distance between them and us, that's all I could think of to do. They would come this way. They had come this way before. That's how we came. Maybe they would split up and search several directions for us. Or maybe they knew where we were and where we were going. I just kept moving, trying to think at the same time. Trying to keep her from falling behind. After a couple of hundred yards, we stopped again. She was in a lot of pain. I didn't know if it was the foot or something else. I was just trying to figure out what to do.

"Grab the water bottle from my backpack and drink it," I told her as I looked around and listened. She needed water. She was badly dehydrated.

Standing there, I realized we couldn't get out the way I had come in. It was a traveled area. Their traveled area. I reached into my pants pocket and felt the wrapper I had picked up back by Silver Creek. But going in the opposite direction would only lead us farther into the wilderness. Farther away from help. And her captors were armed. We were burdened by weight and injury. They could race ahead on the trail and seal off our escape. And then they'd come this way. Find us. Weapons drawn.

By the time she put the water bottle back into my backpack, my legs had gone numb. Dead to the touch, I couldn't even feel them. I was exhausted.

But adrenaline is an amazing thing, and when my eyes saw through a clearing below what I guessed was Wilson Creek, it came to fruition that our best chance of salvation flowed with that water—it had to lead to somewhere.

I began planting my feet firmly into the hillside while she held my hand and followed me downward.

CHAPTER TWENTY-THREE

At the end of an old dirt road somewhere in the White River National Forest at midnight, the van came to a stop. Sarah had no idea where she was or where she was going. She just hurt, and she lay there looking up at the Colorado license plate that had been wedged behind a spare tire along the inside wall of the van. White numbers and letters as big and bold as a childhood book. She tried to drift back into that time of her life. Into her mother's arms.

"Get her out and make sure her mouth is gagged and taped shut," Lowell instructed Kaylee.

Kaylee went around to the back doors of the van and opened them. Sarah lay, cuffed to the floor and pleading for her life. Convinced the end was at hand.

"I don't want any noise from you." Kaylee made her open her mouth, and she stuck a rag in it. She then tightly duct-taped it in place. Running the duct tape twice around the back of her head.

After that, she unlocked the handcuffs and told Sarah to sit up. She put a sweatshirt on her and cuffed her hands behind her back.

"Make sure she can walk at a good pace," Lowell said, turning to get some things together in the front seat.

Sarah looked up at the clear Colorado sky and the Milky Way cluster. The North Star. The air was cold, and it took away the pain in her back without her realizing it. Her legs draped over the bumper of the van as she sat there while Kaylee prepped her for the journey in. Flannel-lined canvas pants that were Kaylee's for many years were yanked up on her and buttoned. Seeing that they fit a little too loosely on her waist, Kaylee fished a bungee cord through the belt loops and was proud of her ingenuity when she solved the problem. After that she put the socks and running shoes back on Sarah and tied them.

"She's ready," Kaylee told Lowell.

Using the van's headlights to see, he had been busy getting the gear out of the van and stowing it into the two packs. Lowell picked up his miner's flashlight and strapped it on his forehead. He then walked around to the back of the van and gave one to Kaylee.

"Get her on her feet," said Lowell as he handed two nylon ropes to Kaylee. "Time to go."

Kaylee put one of them around Sarah's neck and tied the loop. It was tight enough so that it would not slip over her head, loose enough for her to breathe freely. A leash. Kaylee tied the other end of it around her waist and waited for Lowell who had jumped into the van and pulled it off the road and into the brush. When he was far enough in, he got out and began chopping off pine branches with his axe hammer and covered the van with them. Before long it had disappeared. With his feet he kicked the dirt up to disguise the tracks and walked over to the women where Kaylee handed him the second rope, which he also tied around Sarah's neck and his waist. She would be led from the front and the back. Kaylee and Lowell put their packs on and then Lowell strapped his sidearm to his belt. They each made some adjustments on their shoulder straps and began walking.

Lowell led the way as the three of them traveled into the wilderness as though it were the 1700s and they were on their way to a slave ship on the African coast. In the dead of night. Flashlights replacing torches.

It was a brutally long journey for Sarah Evans. Six hours of mountain travel. Arms bound behind her back. Ropes around her neck. Mouth gagged and taped shut. Not knowing. Completely in the dark, in the darkest of worlds.

At daybreak they reached their destination, a small clearing on a mountain ridge above a stream. The wooden remains of what was once a National Forest Service shelter lay on the ground. Nearby there was a stream and a mountain pond, plenty of water around for them to purify and drink. And bathe in. They took off their packs and rested.

Lowell removed the duct tape and gag and sat down next to Sarah to pour water into her mouth. Dehydrated, she was shaking with cold and fear. He put the bottle up to her lips. She knew she needed water, and she accepted it. Stay alive. That was another force battling inside her. Her will to survive.

Fear, death, and survival. Capitulation. Mercy. Suicide. The long day and dark night had scrambled her thoughts. Sitting there, she brought things into view like a windshield slowly defrosting. She had no idea where she was. The time in the van seemed like an eternity. She remembered the AM radio. Thought she heard K something in Colorado come out a speaker in the dash. They were somewhere in the Rockies. That could easily be seen now that the sun was up.

She was sitting with her arms still bound when Lowell removed one of the ropes around her neck. The other rope end was tied to a tree. The two criminals went to work preparing their new homestead. They had packed a tent and a tarp with poles. Sleeping bags. Cooking equipment. Clothes. Rope. Tools. Water purifiers. Propane tanks. Food. Alcohol and weapons.

They erected their communal hut, which they nicknamed "the church," using poles and the tarp. It was tall enough to stand in and wide enough to lay three or four people in. It would provide shade from the sun and shelter from rain without having to get into the tent. On the right side of the church, they put up their tent. Pounded stakes into the ground. Threw in the sleeping bags.

They gathered stones for the imaginary fire pit where they would use propane stoves only to cook their meals. A fire was too risky, its flame and smoke visible for miles. And they used the stones to decorate the church. Kaylee took charge of that. She went down to the stream to find "pretty colored ones," as she called rounded rocks of various hues. She took some of them and shaped an L and S—"Lowell and Sarah"—with them in the center of the church.

With no idea what was going on, Sarah watched all of this as the sun rose and brought with it warmth. She stopped shaking. Her captors were sweating, pausing now and then to stand in the shade of the church.

When they had finally finished setting up the camp, they put their empty packs in the back of the church and piled their tools and weapons on top of them. Keeping them off the ground. Lowell's sidearm remained strapped on his hip, Kaylee's was stowed away in her pack.

"Let's head down to the water and get cleaned up," Lowell said to Kaylee. "Keep hold of her," he instructed, nodding at Sarah.

Kaylee untied the rope that held Sarah in place, then tied it around her waist. Ever vigilant. Kaylee went over to her pack and pulled out two towels, a bottle of shampoo, and a bar of soap. The three of them then made their way down to the stream. When they got there, they undressed. Lowell found another tree and tied Sarah to it. He then got in the water with Kaylee and splashed her. Like children. Smiling. Oblivious to Sarah's ordeal and the frigid mountain water. Shampoo and soap on bodies. Towels, clothes, shoes, and a gun on the rocks on the bank.

"Will you wash her for me?" Lowell asked Kaylee.

Kaylee got out of the water and went over to Sarah. Stood there naked in front of her. "I'm going to remove the handcuffs and rope, let you get cleaned up in the water. You promise you'll be a good girl?"

Taking off her clothes was the last thing she wanted to do, but angering her captors weighed equally upon her. So Sarah said nothing and nodded. She took off her clothes and shoes, and her eyes began to tear up. Kaylee took her by the hand, and she stepped over the rocks in her bare feet and walked into the stream. Lowell tossed the soap to her, and she gave it to Sarah. They stayed right by her in the knee-deep water. He motioned for Sarah to use it. But she couldn't move. She stood there trying not to cry, wishing again she was in her mother's arms. Lowell took the soap out of her hands and started rubbing it all over her body. She was completely numb to the experience. He got excited.

They left the water and then carried their clothes and shoes back up to their campsite. Their bodies clean and as fresh as the new clothes pulled from their packs. Lowell watched Sarah put on Kaylee's underwear and half-length t-shirt that came down just below her chest. He put the rope around her neck and then both of them put on their shoes. Quickly he put on shorts and a T-shirt—never letting go of the rope—and then led Sarah to the church, where Kaylee was waiting.

"It's time," Kaylee said. "We are gathered here to marry this woman to this man." She looked at Sarah and Lowell.

With great horror, Sarah at last realized what this whole thing was about: the church, the rocks, the bath. She was about to become Lowell's wife in her captors' demented minds. Sparking hatred deep within, it brought her back to life. They performed a quick ceremony while Sarah began generating a plan of action.

"And do you, Sarah, take Mr. Daniels to be your lawfully wedded husband?" Kaylee asked.

"I do," Sarah replied.

She looked up at Lowell with willingness in her eyes.

"I now pronounce you man and wife," said Kaylee. "You may kiss the bride."

Bending his muscular six-foot-two-inch frame, Lowell leaned down and kissed Sarah. She kept her lips closed but didn't pull away.

Lowell wrapped his arm around Kaylee's shoulder, and the three of them headed into their tent. Kaylee unzipped it and entered first. Lowell kicked off his boots, ducked inside, and with the rope began pulling Sarah in with him as he stretched out onto his sleeping bag.

But Sarah yanked hard and the nylon slipped from Lowell's hands. It snapped back and flew out of the opening, and then she zippered the tent shut and ran. He was stunned.

For a second or two, he just lay there listening to her footsteps disappear. Knowing she had fooled him. Got the better of him. Then he flew into a rage, grabbing the inside zipper and yanking it hard. It got stuck on the acrylic fabric. He tugged again and again, but it was stuck. So he just grabbed his hands in the small opening and ripped open the door.

Lowell slipped his boots on and went over and grabbed the .38 out of the backpack. Somewhat relieved to see that it hadn't been taken by his departing guest. His sidearm was still attached to his hip, so he gave the .38 to Kaylee who had come out of the tent.

"That little bitch," she said.

"She'll never run again," Lowell vowed. "I promise you that. And after all we went through to get her here. What a waste."

Lowell laced his boots and while low to the ground searched for Sarah's shoe prints. Her running shoes left a distinctive track. He found them leading away from the camp in the direction they had come the night before.

"She's headed back to the road," he said. "You stay here. I'll flush her back this way. Have the handcuffs and gag ready."

He took off running. He was big, strong, and fast. He moved quickly through the mountains and gained on Sarah with every step—propelled by the hunt. It wasn't long until he came upon the jettisoned rope on the trail. He picked it up and continued on.

Sarah was a runner with plenty of stamina, but running on asphalt was different than the rugged terrain of the mountains. Plus the long trek in during the night had taken its toll, and she had yet to replenish her body with the necessary amount of food and water. She fell twice. Skinned her knees and the palms of her hands, which had already been roughed up when the door of the van hit her in the back and slammed her to the road. Drops of blood falling on the ground like bread crumbs for Lowell to follow.

Sweat kept dripping into her eyes and she lost sight of the blurry trail. Lost her way. Lost her composure. Panic set in. It winded her. She stopped to catch her breath and heard them behind her. Heavy breathing. Boots pounding on the dirt. She got up and continued running. Forgetting to pace herself. Winded again, she stopped about a half mile from the camp. Hands and knees still bleeding. Her pursuers sounded closer. She told herself to run but didn't go anywhere. She chose to hide instead. Silence. No sound. Curled up in a ball by some rocks and brush and a fallen pine.

She thought it was both of them that had run past her, but it was only Lowell. She left her hiding place and ran back toward the camp thinking she'd elude them that way. She was running full speed, slightly downhill, when Kaylee jumped out from behind a tree with her .38 drawn.

Sarah was startled and she tripped and fell to the ground while trying to come to a stop. Kaylee rushed her and put the gun to her head and cocked it.

"She's down here," she called out to Lowell.

Moments later Lowell arrived, dripping with sweat. He took his gun and put it to Sarah's face. "I ought to blow your head off," he told her.

"Then do it, you piece of shit," she told him in defiance.

He pulled the gun back, put the rope around her neck, and slapped her across the face. It stung, but she turned her head back to them and spit at both of them. She then started thrashing with her legs. Lowell clamped down tighter. She thought they were going to kill her, and she wasn't going down without a fight.

Lowell flipped her over on her stomach, and Kaylee slapped the handcuffs on her. Her mouth was once again gagged and duct taped. Lowell tightened the rope and it became hard for Sarah to breathe.

"You stop squirming, and I'll take the pressure off so you can breathe. Do we have a deal?" Lowell asked as he pushed the knot firmly against her neck and throat.

Sarah's face turned red. It was horrifying to be choked so she nodded her head yes. She wouldn't squirm, and stopped moving. Lowell gave her a long look and let her suffer for a moment longer before loosening the noose. She gulped in the air.

The three of them sat and rested. They were all tired. When Lowell regained his breath, he got everyone back on their feet.

"Let's go." He yanked the rope and Sarah stumbled forward down the trail. He pulled her up alongside him. "You're going to need to find a new hobby because that was the last time you're ever going to go for a run."

His eyes were narrow and black. What did his words mean? She didn't regret running. She would do it again if the opportunity arose. She would never give up. She would never give up hope of reaching her husband. Her mom and dad. Her siblings. Her friends. They kept the fight alive in her.

When they neared the camp, they detoured south, Lowell was leading the way. They came to a little pond.

"I'm burning up," Kaylee said as she brought her shirt up from her belly to wipe her forehead.

"You're going to regret this," Lowell told Sarah as they stopped by the water. Another warning. A promise. "What a shame, especially after all those years of looking forward to being with you and spending quality time together."

The sun was higher in the sky, and it was becoming a warm summer day. Lowell made Sarah sit against a large boulder, and then he squatted down and began splashing water up on himself. He had Sarah's rope tied firmly around his waist. Kaylee joined him. Sarah found a small, sharp-edged stone and began carving into the boulder with it. With her hands cuffed behind her back, she amazingly wrote from left to right. When she finished, she dropped the stone and began praying in preparation for her last moments on earth.

Kaylee and Lowell finished cooling off, and then yanked Sarah back to her feet. They made their way back to the camp. Lowell tied Sarah's rope to a tree and then walked over to his backpack in the church and grabbed the axe hammer that was on top of it. He then used it to loosen one of the tent spikes and then pulled it from the ground. With the axe hammer and spike, he then searched for a piece of lumber. Something the size of a log for a fireplace. When he found the right piece of wood, he returned to Sarah.

"Untie her from the tree," he told Kaylee. As soon as she was untethered, he thrust the log into Sarah's stomach and she dropped to the ground. "Get on her and hold her down." Kaylee complied. She straddled Sarah's her upper body to prevent her torso and arms from moving. Sarah sensed the imminent danger and as soon as she got her wind back she began kicking. Lowell laid across her legs and put as much of his body weight on them as he could. He then separated Sarah's right leg and put her foot up onto the log. He placed the spike on the top of her foot, and with one quick blow he drove the spike into the top of Sarah's foot. She screamed. The gag pushed beyond capacity. Blood squirting into Lowell's face. He struck it again. And again. And again, until the spike entered the log firmly and rested there.

"I keep my promises," Lowell said, and he dropped the axe and went and sat down in the shade of the church.

Sarah lay unconscious on the ground. Blood pouring out of the top and bottom of her foot. Dripping down the log like the tears on her face.

All day and all night they kept Sarah there as punishment. No food or water. Bound and gagged. A ten-inch tent spike driven through her foot and into a log. The night was horrible. She lay freezing in her T-shirt, and a thin blanket they threw on her. Shivering. Temperatures dropping into the midforties. Hypothermia knocking on the gates. Twenty feet away they drank bourbon while wearing their pants and jackets. They felt nothing for her.

"Where are we going to bury her? This dirt is as hard as rock," Kaylee asked.

"Somewhere down by the stream where it's softer," Lowell replied. "We'll keep her for a few weeks and then do it."

"Then there's no reason to feed her much. We're going to need the food."

They kept her foot nailed to the log for three days while giving her just small amounts of water. Slowly, they were killing her. Her foot became infected. On the third day, in the evening, Lowell removed the spike. The pain was excruciating. He had to loosen it just as he had done when pulling it from the ground below the tent before yanking it out with pliers. Lowell offered to give her some bourbon beforehand if she was willing to take it from his mouth. His offer, which she refused, brought a chuckle from Kaylee and him. Moon up high. Stars above. Clear Colorado night. They were content. Sarah was in hell.

She held on to hope. Those same stars and moon offered her dreams. Dreams of her home. Her husband. Warmth. Help. Freedom. She would not let them go. They were her guardian angels. Eventually they increased the weight of her eyelids until they closed like a theater curtain, and the second act brought the rising sun on stage.

In the morning they strung her up over a Douglas fir branch, as they did each of the following days for the next three weeks, until that moment when our eyes would lock on to each other and she would go free once more.

CHAPTER TWENTY-FOUR

We reached the creek and followed it downstream. I was looking for a place to cross. Full sunlight was on us, which meant we were fully visible. I wanted darkness. Cover. I found a spot that had a nice series of rocks that could act as our bridge. Though the water level was low, the current would easily sweep Sarah off her feet, especially with her one foot so badly injured.

"Hold on to my backpack," I said to her. "I'll go slowly."

I paused before beginning the crossing, thinking that maybe there was no reason to cross the creek. That we could just follow it downstream. But that was too obvious of an escape route. Crossing the fast-moving water was like scaling a prison wall. A barrier. An intimidating one. But beyond it on the other side would bring us more opportunity. So I began placing my feet on the dry tops of the rocks sticking out of the water. About halfway across Sarah slipped. Her right leg went into the water. She tugged me backward for a moment, and I almost lost my balance. I leaned forward to counter her weight to keep me from going into the water.

"Don't let go. I'm going to turn, and then I want you to grab my arm and I'll pull you out," I said loudly in an attempt to be heard over the rushing water. In a quick maneuver, I managed to rebalance myself and turn around and grab her hand. I pulled her right out of the water and onto the rock with me. Her shoe was still on. "Are you OK?"

"Yes. My leg is a little cold. That's all. Sorry I fell."

"You're doing great. We got this," I said, and we continued across the creek.

We made it to the other side, and then reached a grove of aspen trees. It was a good place to stop so that Sarah could get the creek gravel out of her shoe. We were out of view from the upper hillside where we came from. I scanned the mountain looking for any sign of our pursuers. Nothing.

Her foot looked bad, and it was painful for her to put her shoe back on and tie the laces. The water had washed the dried blood off of it, and I could see the infection more clearly. Deep reds, purple, and black. But giving her one more thing to worry about wouldn't do us any good, so I didn't say a thing. I just waited for her to be done so that we could get moving again.

When we stood up, I saw them. They had just come over a ridge. The same ridge Sarah and I had been on. They were on our trail. Following us. I leaned back up against the tree and told Sarah to stay where she was.

"What's wrong?" she asked.

"They're on us." I looked back across the creek and up onto the hillside. Just my head sticking out from the tree.

They were moving quickly. There were two of them. It surprised me to see that one was a woman. Though they were a hundred yards away, they were menacing looking. Each had a gun. Sarah was looking up at me. Again her eyes had fear in them. I looked at her and considered our best option. We wouldn't be able to follow the creek, but it was our only realistic source for finding our way out of the mountains. The forest stretched on forever. Up and over ridges and as far up the peaks its trees could climb without supplemental oxygen. In all directions. The water didn't do that. It went downward through the valley to lower elevation where people built homes and towns. Safety. My home. The girl I loved.

"We have to move away from the creek. We can't follow it along the bank. They'll see us," I told her.

She just kept looking up at me. I couldn't believe the situation I was in. I felt it in my stomach. I was in serious danger. My heart began racing again. My mind trying to figure out what to do next. I hated the thought of leaving the creek, but we had no other choice. They would easily catch up to us if we did that. We had to go deeper into the forest. We would be harder to track. Harder to find. But the farther in we went, the farther it would be to get out.

CHAPTER TWENTY-FIVE

I decided we would head away from the creek and make our way across the valley floor, then head up the mountain range until we could see the creek below. We would parallel it up in the mountains. Be up high enough to follow it from on high. Getting up there, though, was going to be tough. I worried about Sarah's ability to make it. Her foot was more a liability than the weight of my pack.

"I need you to be really tough for me, Sarah." She stood up and I looked back up the hills across the creek. Keeping an eye on them. "We're going to head across this valley as quickly as we can. We'll be able to lose them in the dense forest out there. And then we're going to get up onto those mountains you see in the distance, and we'll follow the creek from up there. Can you do that for me?"

"I will, I can make it. I want you to take me home."

"That's where I want to go too. It's going to take everything we've got to get us there."

I looked down at the ground to make sure we hadn't dropped anything that would mark our trail, and then we got going. We trotted. That was our pace. My heart was pounding as though I was at a full sprint. I was frightened by them. Their ruggedness. Their weapons. I breathed in as much air as possible, trying to regulate my heartbeat. Trying to calm down. So many things ran through my mind while rushing through the trees. Over fallen trunks. On gravel and rocks. Thickets.

She stayed right with me. Step for step like we were a four-legged animal. Sometimes grabbing hold of my backpack and then letting go. A cue to keep going. The farther we traveled, the darker the forest became, and so I knew the sun was sinking below the mountain range we were headed for. It was good to know we weren't meandering. We would be heading up out of the valley floor soon. Climbing in elevation.

Sarah yanked on my backpack, and I stopped. I turned around to face her. Putting my index finger to my lips to let her know to be quiet. To whisper. She wanted water. I gave her just a little bit. It needed to be conserved. There was no way of knowing when or where we would find a source to purify and refill my bottles. Before moving out, we stood silently to see if we could hear anyone behind us. There was nothing but the sound of the forest.

"Let's hope they're looking for us along the creek," I whispered.

Sarah liked the thought and smiled halfway. Just enough to show a little of her two front teeth. Caught me by surprise. It was beautiful and peculiarly soothing. It became easier to breathe. I smiled back at her, and then I turned and we continued on. After a few more minutes, it felt like we were beginning our ascent. I slowed our pace. Better to be moving slowly than to be exhausted and unable to move at all. And I had to worry about the effects of the altitude on her. This wasn't her home. I was certain this was far higher in elevation than what she was used to running in. And her foot. The infection that had set in. I worried that even at a slow pace I was pushing her too hard. It was such a balancing act. It made me stop.

"How are you doing?" I asked.

She looked up at me, and then she bent over and rested with her hands on her knees. "I'm fine," she panted.

"How's your foot?"

"Fine," she replied. "I'm ready when you are."

"Want any water?"

"I can hold off."

She was tougher than I thought.

"It's going to get harder and harder as we start heading uphill. Just let me know when you have to stop."

"I will."

We stayed put for a moment, and I looked back and listened. Nothing. It was a good sign.

CHAPTER TWENTY-SIX

The climb was arduous. It had become twilight without me even noticing, and it became hard to see little rocks that our feet would slip on, or cause our ankles to turn. Small dead limbs that had fallen tripped us. I stumbled, stopped and pointed them out to Sarah. A black bear scrambled away. Startled us. I was thankful for the absence of cubs.

We reached a large, rocky outcrop that we had to traverse. After getting around it, we stopped. It was a good place to rest. We stayed in the trees, not wanting to expose our silhouettes. The sun had gone down behind the mountains. I looked down into the valley to see if I could spot the creek. Or the beam of a flashlight near it. Just darkness.

I wondered where they were. I wondered if we were in a safe place. It was getting almost too dark to continue on. It was a hard choice. Stay or go. I liked being up above the valley floor. We would definitely continue on that line. A constant vantage point. But we would have to be able to see the creek. Follow it out.

"I think we should just stay where we are for tonight," I said to Sarah.

Looking at her it was obvious she wanted to keep going. Keep going until she was home. Spending another night in these mountains was like staying an extra day in hell to her. She had had enough of this place. But it really was our only choice. We would need flashlights to keep moving, and those lights would only act as beacons to those seeking us. The mountains would also become much colder in a few hours. Possibly dropping thirty or forty degrees. It was clear out, and the warmth of the day would just evaporate away. No clouds to act like a blanket for us and keep the air warm. Plus our sweat was beginning to dry, and we risked hypothermia if we remained exposed.

"I can go on if that's what you really want to do," she replied. "Please don't stop because you think this is as far as I can go."

"It's not you. I promise. It's just gotten too dark to go any farther. There's no way they'll find us in this darkness. So we're safe here."

"But what about in the morning?"

"We'll move on in the morning and stay ahead of them."

"How do we know where they are?" She was still full of fear and anxiety. And I had plenty of it too.

"It's more important that they don't know where we are. It's going to be OK. I'll get you home."

I took off my backpack and began getting our area ready for the night. For sleeping. Level ground the length of our bodies. No rocks. Just hard dirt. I unhooked the bungee cords that held my sleeping bag and sleeping pad to the outside of the bottom of my backpack and laid them on the ground. The down bag on top of the pad.

"Welcome to the Holiday Inn," I said in an attempt at humor to calm her down. She smiled.

"Do you need me to help you with anything?" she asked.

"No, I've got it."

The backpack was up by where our heads would be, and I took out some of the food I had. We were both hungry. We ate trail mix and a couple of candy bars and then washed it down with some water. Our water was running low.

"You're going to need to put on some of my clothes for the night. Is that OK?" I asked.

"Yes, thank you." She had already begun to get cold.

"They're going to be a little big on you, but they'll keep you warmer than what you have on."

The temperature was rapidly dropping. In the middle of summer, that's how the Rockies are:sweat and sunburns during the day and chilly at night.

I turned my head so she could take off her shorts to put on my jeans and a fleece pullover. I put her shorts in my backpack. They would keep her cool in the hot sun tomorrow. My pants were way too big to stay up on her, and she just stood there holding them up. Her outline in the post twilight sky. I put on my long-sleeve thermal shirt and offered her a fresh pair of socks. Warm feet. She unlaced her shoes and began to put on the socks. I heard her wince. I knew it was her foot.

"Let me take a look at your foot, Sarah."

"It's fine," she replied.

"I won't touch it or do anything to it. I promise. I just want to look at it."

"But we can't turn the light on."

"It won't shine through the sleeping bag."

I didn't know if her hesitation was the fear of exposing our position or the fear of what we might see. There was also the real fear of someone who wasn't medically trained poking around and doing more harm than good. We were both aware of that, and that was the last thing I would do. I just had to see what was going on because everything depended on our ability to travel. To travel for miles over rough terrain.

She sat down on my backpack and slipped her foot into the sleeping bag. When it was deep inside, I leaned over and reached down with the flashlight. The colors were the first thing I noticed. Blue, red, and a big, black bull's eye covering the top of the foot and extending up her leg. Grotesque and alarming. Without me asking, she turned it so that I could see the bottom as well. It looked the same.

"Why is there a wound on the top and bottom?" I asked and Sarah began to cry. Her tears came right off her cheeks and onto my backpack. "I'm sorry. I didn't mean to upset you."

She wiped away tears. Dried her face with the front and back of her hand.

"It's okay. It's not your fault," she said. "They did it to me."

"What did they do?"

She took a deep breath, and it was obvious that whatever it was it was hard for her to talk about. The problem either way was that I had only a few basic medical supplies with me: an ace bandage, Band-Aids, and Neosporin. I gently dabbed it on the top and bottom wounds and covered them with Band-Aids. I did what I could, knowing she needed much more.

The two of us climbed into the sleeping bag. As awkward as it could've been for two strangers to do this, I never gave it a second thought, and she didn't appear to either. A tight fit. We lay on our sides. The down and our bodies keeping each other warm. The shorts and long-sleeve shirt I wore were plenty for me in the down bag. But I knew she needed as much clothing as possible because her infection would possibly affect her core body temperature. I would rather she be too hot than too cold. We were body to body.

Shape to shape. The backpack up by our heads. Our shoes there as well.

Neither of us spoke. Just the sounds of the forest. The night was black. The trees were so thick that the sky wasn't visible. Darkness was our friend. We were invisible like two kids hiding in a closet, and that brought me comfort.

There were so many things that I wanted to know, but I would let her tell me when the time was right. When she felt like it. So I just lay there. Running things through my head. Thinking about them. Wondering how far they would search the creek before realizing we weren't there. It was hard for me to gauge how much distance we had put between them and us. It felt like we had traveled far. But they were strong and healthy, and they were unencumbered. They could go all night. But maybe they would give up. Let us go. Cut their losses and run. I couldn't convince myself of that though, and I lay there just thinking of everything. Missing Erin.

"Alex," Sarah said in her softest of voice.

"I'm right here," I whispered back to her.

"I want to tell you everything," she said. "You need to know."

She began her story, but was so fatigued that she soon fell asleep. And so my story remained untold as well. To her, I remained just a fly fisherman in search of rising trout. That's all she had to know. It was better that way.

CHAPTER TWENTY-SEVEN

I opened my eyes and wondered if I was still sleeping. The night was so black under the trees in the forest. But they began to adjust and reveal the outline of the landscape around us. I lay still on my side not wanting to awaken Sarah, listening to the steady rhythm of her breathing. Her back expanding into my chest and then retreating. After a while though, I became restless and thought it would be wise to be vigilant once more. I quietly unzipped the sleeping bag and slid out of the womb. It was cold out and I felt it right away on my legs. I slipped on my boots, without bothering to tie them, then I made my way out of the trees. When I reached the clearing where the slope of the mountain greatly increased in grade, I could see much of the valley below.

There was no detail, just darkness down there. I covered the entire area with my eyes and saw nothing that posed a threat. There was a large rock and I sat down on it and took up my post. The cold keeping me alert. A shooting star caught my attention and I watched it fall behind the mountains across from me. Then another one. And another one. They were so fast. I tried to lead them like skeet. One of them looked like it fell into the valley, and that's when I saw their lights. I stood up and looked long and hard down into those trees. Darkness, darkness, darkness, light. Darkness, darkness, light. Repeating over and over. It was them. I knew it in my gut, and they were weaving their way through the trees with their flashlights to guide them. Coming toward us. I left my post and went to awaken Sarah.

"Sarah, wake up." I shook her left shoulder. It took a couple of times to get her to come to.

"What?" she replied, without any movement in our sleeping bag.

"We have to get going," I whispered.

"Is something wrong?"

She could hear it in my voice. "I think they may have picked up our trail. I need you to start getting ready. I'll be right back."

"Where are you going?"

"I'm just going to check out the valley again. I'll be right over here. I'm not going anywhere," I said. She was frightened to be left alone in the dark.

Over at the clearing and looking down below, I definitely saw them. Lights. On and off. A mile away, two at the most. Flickering as they weaved between the trees. They were heading our way.

It was them. Had to be. They were tracking us. I felt fear and anger at the same time. Anger at their relentless pursuit of us. No rest. They weren't going to stop. I was cold and tired. Willing to think about making a stand. But fatigue can lead to costly decisions. We had no chance against them. I let the cold air clear my mind. We would not be foolish. We were ahead of them, and if we lightened our load then we could move even faster. Stay ahead. I had to get rid of the coke. That would make my pack forty pounds lighter. Bury it somewhere. I could always come back and get it.

I hurried to Sarah. My eyes had adjusted well to the darkness, and I could see outlines and shapes. She was sitting up in the sleeping bag. I squatted down right next to her and began tying my boots.

"Sarah, we have to get going. They're following us down in the valley."

"You saw them?"

"I saw their flashlights. I'm certain it's them, and they're coming this way."

"But you couldn't actually see them, right?"

"No, I couldn't. It's too dark, and they're too far away," I replied honestly. But I knew it was them.

"Then maybe its people looking to rescue us. Maybe it's the police or search and rescue people," she said.

She had gotten excited with the possibility that these lights were the light at the end of our tunnel. But I knew it was false hope.

"I don't think these are the good guys, Sarah."

"But you don't know for sure."

"No, I don't know for sure, but I do know that search and rescue, the police, the sheriff, or just volunteers who would be out at night looking for you would be calling out your name with megaphones or something like that, and there would be a big group of them," I told her.

She had gotten out of the sleeping bag and winced in pain when she stood up and put weight on her foot. We were both standing. Looking at each other. She was thinking about things. We didn't have much time, but I gave her the opportunity to let it all sink in. Just as I had done. The cold air bringing us to our senses.

"That's them down in the valley coming for us," I said firmly. "They know these mountains and we've got to get out of here."

"I'm sorry," Sarah said, and she hugged me. I had gotten through to her. It was tough letting her down, but it was time to get moving.

"It's OK, it's OK. I need to get rid of some things in my pack. It will be much lighter, and we'll be able to move a lot quicker. Can you roll up the sleeping bag for me and make sure my pants are tight enough to stay up on you? Here's my belt."

"Thanks."

"And you'll probably have to roll the pant legs up too."

I grabbed the backpack and made my way to the back side of the rocky outcrop. Though I knew it was risky to turn on the flashlight, it was absolutely necessary so that I could see what I was doing. Forty pounds of coke was an expensive thing to bury and hide, and I wanted to do it right. The best I could under the circumstances. I waited until I was fully on the back side of the outcrop before turning on the light, and even then I kept it muted with my shirt. There was a ledge about ten feet up that had partially rounded rocks the size of bowling balls on it. There was also a baby pine growing out of it that was a good landmark. Some dirt. I looked in other directions and shone the light, but no place looked as good as the ledge. Quickly I scrambled up the outcrop and set my backpack on the ledge.

"Where are you?" Sarah's voice whispering to me in the night.

"I'll be right there."

There were four or five good size rocks behind the pine that I picked up and moved to the side temporarily. Good dirt underneath. My hands spaded and splintered the earth. As quickly as I could. Removing the dirt like two small plastic shovels on a beach. It didn't take long to dig the hole. The coke all wrapped up in layers of plastic lowered into it. The dirt put back in and covering it up. All cavities filled. Rocks crowning the top. It was well hidden.

The pack was now unbelievably light. Barely knew I was carrying it. I held on to the flashlight but turned it off and went to Sarah. She had turned up the pant legs of my jeans, and the belt was cinched tight. My fleece pullover draping down just below her thighs. She was warm and could move. That was all that mattered.

She had rolled up the sleeping bag and pad and held them in her arms for me. I took off my backpack, strapped them onto it with the bungee cords, and then returned it to my shoulders and waist. It still felt light. We would be able to move as quickly as her abductors. As long as her foot held out.

"Ready to go?" I asked, while keeping hold of the flashlight. Muting it with my shirt I looked at my watch. It was 4:10 a.m. I was surprised that we had slept that long.

Sarah nodded her head that she was ready, and then I went over once more to quickly check the valley. The lights were getting closer. I also looked up at the outcrop and studied the area as best I could. I wanted to photograph it in my mind. The outcrop. The view of the valley. I would need to come back and get the coke at some point. I would need to find it. Deliver it as promised.

The clear skies offered just enough light to put one foot in front of the other. We had no other choice. In and out of the trees. Following the ridge line as best we could while gradually descending. Keeping the valley to our right. The creek that was down there somewhere flowing to our exit. No sign of lights in the valley. We were either making good progress, or they had reached the hillside and had begun ascending. That would put them out of our view. Eventually they would be directly in line with us. Then behind us. Following the arch of our trail.

They put no effort into disguising their approach. Lights were on. Maybe they wanted us to know that they were on our trail, hoping we would panic, make a mistake. Whatever their intentions, they had forced us to travel at night which gave them the advantage. They were using lights and we were virtually traveling blind.

But our advantage was our will. Our lives. We had made it this far. It was clear that when needed we could find a way to stay ahead of them, and that was what I tried to focus on. But my mind was so busy trying to navigate through the dark forest it was hard to think of anything.

Sarah fell. Then stumbled again. I stopped each time, helped her up. Made sure she was okay and then continued on. It was tough on her, but she never complained. She did her best hanging on to my backpack and keeping up with me. Then she went down hard. There was a thud, and she moaned.

"Are you alright?" I asked. Her body just a shadow against the mountain. The first hint of morning started to illuminate the lower sky bordering the peaks.

"I feel sick," she replied, and she remained in a fetal-like position.

"You need more water."

"No. I don't want anything to drink."

She pulled herself up onto all fours, and began vomiting. What little food she had in her system came out. And then it was just dry heaves followed by a sudden collapse and her body's return to the pebbles, sticks and dirt. She was in misery, and it terrified me as I realized the gravity of our situation. We were not moving, and every second counted. I was certain that I would soon hear them.

"I really think you need water, Sarah."

She didn't reply. More dry heaves at ground level. She began crying. I reached down to pull her hair out of her face and touched her forehead. It was really hot. Beyond just being warm from the physical exertion. She had a bad fever.

I took off my pack and grabbed a water bottle. There wasn't much left in it, but it would be enough to help her.

"Please take a sip," I said, lowering the bottle near her mouth.

Again no reply. Stomach in and out. Not even enough energy to get up on all fours. Darkness decreasing. She was coming into view much more clearly. When she lifted her head and looked up at me, I saw the intensity of pain in her eyes. Just a glimpse. And then her head went back down. Hair dangling. And then she dropped back down onto the ground. Curling up.

"Sarah, what's going on?" I asked her with as much sympathy and despair as I had ever felt.

"I can't go on," she said, barely getting the words out.

"Can I take off your shoe to look at your foot?"

I didn't wait for her reply. It was fast becoming too perilous of a situation to allow for democracy. It hurt her for me to even untie her shoe. When I slipped it off, she moaned in agony. Disregarding the care for revealing our position, I turned on the flashlight and looked at her foot with the Band-Aids still there. It was hideous: black-and-blue and swollen. Bright red and purple going far up her leg. The infection had spread. She was seriously ill from it. The high fever. The vomiting.

My heart began pounding. I didn't know what to do. Panic set in. I was in over my head. I kept thinking about them gaining on us.

"Sarah, we have no choice but to keep moving. They will find us if we stay here," I said directly, as though I was unconsciously trying to break my bond from her if needed.

"Go on without me," she said, heaving up again. Nothing came out. There was nothing left in her.

She was giving me a way out, which made it even tougher for me.

"I can't leave you here."

"I'm dying, and there's no reason for you to die with me."

"We're not going to die, Sarah. You've come this far. I know we can find our way out of here today and find someone to help us. We're almost home. Look, the sun is coming up." I pointed to the peaks in the distance, which were beginning to glow.

She made no attempt to embrace the arriving day. Motionless, she lay on her left side, curled up. The side of her head and face rested on and pine needles and dirt. I reached down and again touched her forehead. She was burning up. I poured the remaining water in my second bottle on her forehead and then onto her lips.

I couldn't understand how this was happening. She had been with me step for step. There were the stumbles and some falls, but she had not given me any true indication of the severity of the condition she was in. She had probably been in much more pain than she ever let on. It couldn't have come on this rapidly. She was so much tougher than I'd realized. And then I began feeling guilty. Had I pushed her too hard? The infection overtaking her because her body was physically exhausted and her immune system lacked any punch.

"Sarah, I can carry you," I said, realizing I could never leave her. "We'll leave the pack behind, and we'll find a safe place to hide." No way could I just walk away and leave her to die.

There was no response. I rubbed her head. Running my hand through her hair. Tears started to run off my cheeks, and my eyes began to blur. She turned her head to look up at me.

"Tell my husband and my mom and dad that I love them so much, and I'm so sorry for all this," she said, exerting a tremendous amount of effort to get out the words.

I gently rubbed her head. "You don't need to be sorry for anything."

"Thank you for helping me." She turned to rest her head back on the ground and began talking incoherently. "The rock," I heard her say faintly, and then "number," and then more words I couldn't understand. I began crying. I lay next to her and wrapped her in my arms. The two of us. Alone. I hugged her and felt her breathing becoming more erratic.

"Hang on, Sarah. Just hang on."

She stopped breathing. Her eyes shut. I held her as tight as I could and wept like a baby. Curled up around her. She died in my arms, and only for a few moments more was I able to lie there with her and hold her.

My tears stopped the instant I heard them. Their voices were close. They were talking excitedly to each other. Instincts kicked back in. Her body had quickly turned cold from death and the morning chill, and I let go of it. Let go of her. I never thought I could leave her. Never. But I had no choice.

"Sarah, Sarah," called a woman's eerie, strange, childlike voice.

I quickly stacked three rocks by her head to mark the gravesite, threw on my backpack, and took off running. My fly rod and case, which was nothing more than a three-foot-long aluminum tube strapped above my sleeping bag, came flying off and began rolling down the side of the hill. In my panic I just let it go and kept on going. I could hear that weird woman calling out Sarah's name. I ran and ran. Forgetting to pace myself. In complete panic. Just running. One of them saw me, aimed and fired a revolver.

CHAPTER TWENTY-EIGHT

Erin never slept well when Alex was gone. The bed felt empty without him. She had gotten up a few times during the night. Sitting there on her side of the bed with her knees to her chest. Smoking a cigarette. The lamp turned on low. Just sitting there thinking. Then back to bed. Back to sleep. Restless. Finally she went into a deep sleep after getting up and going to the bathroom around six o'clock. She saw the light of daybreak peeking in through the curtains as she pulled the bed sheet over her. There was something comforting to her about this morning's sunlight, and it eased her mind. Sleep took over once more.

The buzzer rang and rang. It awakened Erin, and she just lay there hoping it would stop and whoever it was would just go away. The clock read 10:20 a.m., and she was surprised at how long she had been sleeping. Wearing Alex's T-shirt and bunny slippers, she walked out of the bedroom and into the living room where the intercom for the front door to their building was.

"Who is it?" she asked while pressing the white button.

"It's Carter."

"Hey, Carter, come on in." She pressed the button to allow him into the twelve-unit building.

She heard him coming up the steps and waited by the door. She opened it when he reached the landing. Right away she noticed that he did not look like his normal relaxed self. He was tense. There was no warm welcome from him like he usually extended. And he was more casually dressed than normal. His gray polo shirt wasn't tucked into his army-green hiking shorts, and his jean jacket was rarely seen in summer. It looked as though he'd just put on the first things he grabbed from his closet and dresser. Unusual for him. And it was even stranger that he would just be stopping by on a Saturday morning.

The door swung open, and Erin invited him in. He immediately reached into his coat pocket, pulled out a cigarette, and lit it. She grabbed a blanket from the back of the couch and wrapped herself up in it. The open kitchen window had let in the cool morning air, and she also realized that the T-shirt she had on may be more revealing than she wanted.

"What's up, Carter? Are you OK?"

The two of them sat down in the small living room. He took the couch, and she took the white wicker chair across from it. With the big pillows. It was where she always sat. Legs folded up Indian style.

He took a drag from his cigarette and blew out the smoke. Looking at her. Saying nothing. Wondering what she knew.

"Okay, Carter. Are you just going to sit there? What's going on?"

He took another drag and then leaned forward. She had never seen him like this before, and it made her lean back in her chair away from him.

"Do you know where Alex is, and I need you to tell me the truth."

"What are you talking about? And what do you mean 'tell you the truth?'" She paused and gave him a look that let him know that she didn't like being talked to like a little schoolgirl. "He went fishing. Didn't you drop him off at that trail he was talking about?"

He kept looking at her. Looking at her eyes. Searching for the truth.

"If you know where Alex is, then you need to tell me. This is serious, Erin."

"Carter, tell me what's going on. Has something happened to Alex?" she said, sitting up perfectly straight. He studied her closely, convinced that she didn't know any more than he did regarding Alex's whereabouts. He could see she wasn't lying.

"I don't know. I honestly don't. But there's something you need to know, and what I'm going to tell you doesn't leave this room. OK?"

"Yes, I promise."

"Alex didn't go fishing. He was running coke for me, and he was supposed deliver it to this guy, but he never showed up."

A pit formed in the bottom of Erin's stomach. Both from being lied to and from finding out the truth. There was resentment too, and most of it was directed at Carter for getting Alex involved. But her fear for Alex outweighed anything else.

"So what are you saying? Tell me Alex is okay."

His reply only heightened her anxiety. "I can't tell you something I don't know."

"Then tell me what you do know."

Carter obviously would have preferred to keep Erin in the dark about the coke. Coke that didn't belong to him, but yet he would ultimately be held accountable for. But seeing her worried, he knew he had no option before she started looking for answers elsewhere.

"Again, this doesn't leave this room, Erin."

"It won't."

"Then just listen to me and try not to ask too many questions. I've been flying coke into Aspen for a few years. Lately though there have been some busts, so I decided to take extra precautions, and that's why I hired Alex to hike it in to a lake and deliver it to my contact."

"Is this what he did the last time he said he was going fishing and you dropped him off?"

"Yes," said Carter, as he saw the mounting anger in her face. "The problem is that the people who I fly the stuff in for said Alex never showed up, and they want to know where he is. More importantly to them, they want to know where their coke is. This is serious stuff, Erin."

"Why did you get him involved in this?"

"It was just one of those things. I hadn't planned on it. But that's not what matters at this point. We need to locate Alex."

"What if something has happened to him? What if he's hurt? We need to go find him right now," Erin said, standing up.

"Just sit down for a second." She did as he asked. "We both want to find him. It's my neck too. But we can't just go running all over the place. For obvious reasons it's got to be low-key."

"You can't ask me to sit around and wait."

"That may not be what you want to do, but that's what you have to do. I was scheduled to pick him back up at the trailhead later today, and that's where I plan to go. It won't help anything having you there with me. If he doesn't show up, then we'll talk some more."

"What do you think happened to him?"

"I have no idea," he replied. "We are dealing with a lot of money here, Erin, and some people might just be tempted enough to walk away with it."

"Maybe so, but Alex isn't that type of guy. He wouldn't do that to you, and he wouldn't do that to me."

"I wouldn't think so either. But I've learned that people are capable of just about anything."

He was able to put a little question mark in Erin's head, especially since this was something that Alex had kept from her. He had lied to her. Not just about something little.

"How much coke does Alex have with him?" Erin asked, trying to further assess the situation.

"I really don't want to talk about the details. I think I've given you enough for now."

"No, I think you need to tell me more."

Carter paused, looked away from her, and then turned back and looked her in the eye.

"Why don't you ask Alex yourself when he gets back?"

"Alex didn't walk away with your blow, Carter. Something's wrong. Something has happened."

"I'm going to go wait for him as planned. I'll be back as soon as I can. With or without him. And one last thing—just stay here and don't answer the door for anyone but me."

Erin read between the lines, and when Carter got up to leave she followed him to the door and then locked it with the deadbolt after he was gone. She went back to her chair and sat down and ran every scenario she could think of through her mind.

However, the truth was something she could never have imagined.

CHAPTER TWENTY-NINE

I was running away from Sarah's body at a full sprint while the bullet honed in. Faster than the speed of sound, I felt it before I heard it. Hitting the aluminum frame of my backpack like a lightning bolt. Thrusting me forward down the hill, head over heels. A somersault and landing smack on my ass. Full of adrenaline, I never even stopped. I sprang back up to my feet and continued running. Never looking behind. Sweat pouring out my left shoulder and down my back.

Traveling alone I reached the valley floor in no time at all. The terrain leveled out. No longer heading downhill. Without as much momentum, I began to slow. My strides shortened. But I kept going. Strong. Sucked in each breath. Filling my lungs with mountain air. Arms and legs in tune as I glided between those trees. Over those little boulders, fallen limbs.

The impact of the bullet sounded like an explosion, and it remained ringing in my ears. It was all I could hear racing as fast as I could through the valley, putting as much distance as I could between me and them. By the time my hearing fully returned, I had begun to level my speed off at a medium-paced jog. Sometimes even converting to a fast walk. And then back to jogging. I refused to stop.

Daylight had come. As much as it was welcomed, it was also feared. I was fully visible once again. And with the light came the reality of what had just happened. I stopped and wondered how long I'd been running, and while standing there noticed the back of my left shoulder feeling like it had been stung by a wasp. It itched and burned. I lifted up on the strap on my pack in an attempt to itch it. Did it twice. Then pain began setting in. I reached back behind my shoulder and slid my hand under my shirt and pack. It hurt to touch it. It was sweaty too. When I brought my hand out, I saw the blood.

I took my backpack off and saw where the bullet had hit the frame, tearing a hole in the nylon material of the pack on its way there. It was right where the upper crossbar and side bar were joined by a screw. The screwhead was flattened, and the frame was indented, and a piece of it the size of a tooth filling had been chipped off. I couldn't believe the frame was still together. But I then began to worry about where the bullet had gone. I reached back under my shirt where the pain was. Where the blood was. Lightly feeling around. It was tender and still burned.

I began fearing the worst. That the bullet had lodged into my back just below my shoulder. Again I reached back there and felt around. The wound did not seem to be large. About the size of the tip of my baby finger. For a minute I kept my fingers on the wound. Applying pressure. This also helped the pain subside. My left arm was able to move in all directions, and movement with my back and left side was not restricted. A good sign. I began rationalizing that maybe the bullet never hit me. Maybe it was just a chip of the frame that got knocked off by the bullet and stuck in me. And the bullet just ricocheted off the frame and missed me. It made perfectly good sense. I was OK. Lucky perhaps.

From the looks of my hand, the bleeding had decreased. I knew part of it was because my heart rate had slowed down, but I had convinced myself that my wound was minor and that the bullet had missed me. I had caught a break. Looking behind me, I waited and could hear them in the distance. The voices. I took off running.

It was a footrace. All I had to do was stay ahead of them. Physically I was capable now of doing that. Without the weight of the coke, without Sarah, the playing field had been somewhat leveled, though I wished I had a firearm. Protection. As long as I stayed on a direct path of some sort, ahead of them, and not running in circles, which had become my biggest concern, then I should be able to escape them. The creek had to be up ahead, and then I would follow it out. Back to my original plan. I would be with Erin soon. God, how I missed her.

And then thinking of her began to worry me as I kept a steady pace. As the underbrush became thicker. I noticed the aspens mingling with the conifers. And more and more shrubs and bushes. Berry plants. It took more concentration to blaze my trail, and my thoughts rotated between what I needed to do with my arms and legs to maintain my forward progress, and the danger I had put Erin in. We were dealing with a drug cartel, and they would be knocking on Carter's door. Erin would be their best chance of getting to me. She was in harm's way. All my thoughts turned to her. I had to reach her.

CHAPTER THIRTY

She saw the pickup truck through the kitchen window. There were two men in it. Sitting in the cab. Engine off. Windows down. It was an older truck. Off-white in color. It was parked on the side of the road across from their building's parking lot. Erin had a lateral view of them, broadside. The driver wore a white sleeveless shirt, which accentuated his deeply tanned skin around his shoulder. A brown-and-white baseball hat sat on his head of long black hair. His elbow rested on the door where the window cranked down into, while his hand and fingers extended to the roof. The other man could only be seen when he leaned forward for the ashtray. They were talking to each other and periodically glancing over toward the apartment building.

Afraid, Erin moved away from the window. It was odd for the truck to be parked there without any construction work going on in the area. For them to be just sitting in it. She went to the phone and dialed Carter's number. He didn't pick up. She tried it again. Still no answer. He had instructed her to stay in the apartment and to not answer the door, but she wasn't the type to wait around. She tried his place one more time, and when he didn't answer, she grabbed her purse and keys and left the apartment. Locking the door behind her and checking it.

Down the steps and out into the parking lot she walked to her car. On her way she looked over at the truck. They didn't lock eyes. She got into her Cherokee and drove out of the parking lot. Through her sunglasses she got a good look at them as she turned onto the street. They looked at her. She was a pretty girl, so that wasn't uncommon. In her rearview mirror she saw that they had Colorado plates. She didn't know if that was good or bad. Still trying to figure things out.

Her heart sank when she looked into the rearview mirror again and saw that the truck had begun moving. She made a left turn onto Gillespie and kept glancing into the rearview mirror. Hoping the truck wouldn't turn too. But it did. They kept their distance, but she was certain now that she was being followed. She slowed up and let them get closer to her and then made a quick turn onto Fifth. A final test. They did the same. She sped up and thought about what to do. The police station wasn't far away, and she would certainly find protection there. But she was concerned about the consequences that might have for Alex. She drove up to Highway 82 and took it toward Snowmass. Heading out of town.

Two cars had gotten in between her and the pickup. She saw this as her chance, and she accelerated. As the traffic thinned out farther from town there were fewer cars for her to pass, and she thought she had put some distance between her and the truck. When she saw the sign for the airport, she made the decision to turn in there.

She pulled into the parking lot at a high speed. Dangerously fast. Narrowly missing a woman who was wheeling her suitcase to her car. She drove to the end of the parking area and backed into an empty space. Sitting there looking for the truck. There was no sign of it on 82, and only an Audi with a woman behind the wheel turned into the airport during her ten minutes of waiting. When she convinced herself that she had lost them, she raced home. Nervously keeping an eye out along the way.

It was a huge relief when there was no sign of them or their truck at the apartment. Up the stairs she went. Two at a time. Keys rattling in her hand like pockets full of change. Once inside she bolted the door and went to the window. Still no truck. Deep breaths. Calming herself down. When her breathing settled she went and picked up the phone by the kitchen counter and dialed Carter. This time, he answered.

"Carter, where the hell have you been? I've been trying to reach you all day."

"They called me and told me about your little field trip, Erin."

"You mean you know the guys who are following me," she said incredulously.

"Yes. Have you forgotten that your boyfriend is missing with something valuable and the people that it belongs to want to know where it is? I told you not to leave the apartment."

"Why didn't you tell me you were going to have someone parked outside of my apartment watching me?"

"Listen, Erin. Some of this is not my doing. As I said, the people who own it want it back, and they are going to do everything in their power to get it. And if that means having someone follow you to see where you go, to see if you may eventually come in contact with Alex, if you know what I'm saying, then they're going to do that. I can't stop them. And honestly, maybe it's not a bad thing, especially since you drove to the airport. You don't exactly look innocent."

Carter could not be trusted. It was clear that the money and coke was all that mattered. She and Alex were second.

"I have to go. I'll call you later," she told him, hanging up.

CHAPTER THIRTY-ONE

Rushing water was the sound of freedom. It was just up ahead. Through the thickets. An artery near the top of the world beginning its pilgrimage to the sea. Water seeking its own level. And there I was in that valley, laying my eyes upon it like the lifeline that it was. I had just come through the remainder of the golden currant shrubs and was standing on the banks of what I thought was Wilson Creek. The same creek I had crossed the day before with Sarah. I was certain it was the same one, running right through the heart of this valley. Leading somewhere.

It was amazing how much happiness it brought me. Hope. Relief. Liquid for my body and soul. I took off my backpack and pulled out my water purifier and bottles.

Fresh water had never tasted so good. Feeling it running down my throat. Standing there watching the water rush past me, its coolness under the hot mountain sun.

The bank was lined with bushes and trees and was somewhat steep. It was not a good highway, but off I went. Just like I had been doing. Back through the thick shrubs away from the creek and then finding the easier route downstream under the cover of the aspens and pines. Avoiding the thorn bushes that had grown fond of my arms and legs. I was moving well. The rushing water over to the right just a small distance away. My guide. Sometimes the water would come into view. And then disappear. After a few minutes the terrain dropped away, and the creek flowed into a small canyon. I cut back down to the bank and stuck to the steep shoreline. This was easier than climbing up and out of the canyon. And it ensured that I would be following the water. At one point the bank became so steep, my only choice was to enter the water. Knee high. The freestone creek with snowmelt as its source numbing my legs instantly like so many of the trout streams I enjoyed free-wading with my fly rod in hand. The connection of the cold water to the skin like the cold blood inside the trout, linking us together.

As I hugged the bank, I heard something above the sound of the rushing water. I stopped. Waited. Then I heard it again. It was voices. *Boom, boom, boom* my heart started pounding. Waist deep in the water with the canyon wall to my back and the shoreline they were moving

down to my right. The whitewater between us. I had no-
where to go. They were coming quickly because their
voices became much easier to hear over the rapids and
the wildly beating drum inside me. I saw a crease in the
canyon wall marked by shadow a few yards downstream
and I hurried there. Careful not to slip. The indentation
was just enough for me to squeeze back into. I pushed in,
into the darkness as far as I could with my backpack on.
Standing sideways out of the sunlight by a body width or
two. My head turned toward the bank to look for them.
To look them in the eye when they aimed and fired. It
had to be coming.

He had a large shiny revolver in his hand and he was
running upriver. It stunned me to see that somehow the
man had gotten ahead of me. Then the woman came running along the bank from upstream with her gun firmly
in her grip. They obviously had separated in an attempt to
box me in. I couldn't believe the skill they had. I stopped
breathing and held my breath as though I were under water and not above it. In the darkness of that crack in the
canyon wall, I was as motionless and invisible as I could
possibly be. They were fifty feet away, together, and looking in all directions.

Several times they glanced right at me while turning
their heads, but their eyes never picked me out of the shadows. They started talking. I couldn't hear their words but
saw expressions of confusion and anger. The man pointed
upstream with his weapon, and they started off in that

direction. Five steps and they were out of my line of sight. I began breathing again.

I waited ten minutes. Not moving a muscle and counting to sixty, ten times. *One one-thousand, two one-thousand, three one-thousand.* I inched my way out to where I could see upstream and downstream as far as the river traveled before bending out of view. There was no sign of them. The water was too deep and fast to cross. The closest place to get to the opposite bank, and up and out of the water and into the shelter of the trees, was upstream. The direction they had gone. The direction I didn't want to go. But I had no choice. I went as fast as I could. Going against the strong current which exhausted me. Looking all around for them, but also having to watch where I placed my feet. Avoiding the moss-covered stones. I reached a shallow area and forded the stream. Crawled up the bank and ran into the woods. Waiting silently in the thick brush like grouse. *One one-thousand. Two one-thousand.*

When I convinced myself that I had escaped their trap, I exited my hiding place and took off downriver back in the tree line. Running, running and running. Each step to the boom of my heart.

On and on I went, and somehow it had become four in the afternoon. I looked at my watch twice to make sure the second hand was moving. The sun overhead confirmed everything. It was well past its zenith. I hadn't even noticed. There was still plenty of daylight left, but at some point I was going to have to make a decision on when and where to stop and lay low for the night.

When daylight began fading the terrain became no-
ticeably more rugged. More challenging. Then came the
climb up the hill. The ascent was gradual at first but soon
became steep. The forest was still so thick and the light
so diminished that I couldn't see what was up in the distance. There was no vantage point. Just trees and rocks,
everything else had begun to look the same. It was hard
to tell if I was going up a hill or a mountain. There was
no way of knowing. My head stayed down, looking at the
placement of my feet. Each one landing in a good, firm
spot. Pushing off and repeating the process. It became
more and more drudging. My energy and enthusiasm
draining from my mind and body like the perspiration
running down from my forehead and off the tip of my
nose. Drops sometimes hitting the front of my boots.

I went up the hill as far as I could. My day was done.
Completely spent. I swung my pack off and sat on the
ground. Because of the slope, I had to dig my heels in
to keep from sliding. Looking down, I saw how far I had
come. Looking upward, I could see how far I still had to
go. And beyond. It was a long way up, and so I was content
with the decision to stay put. The climb would be there
waiting for me in the morning. It felt so good to just sit
there. My feet were tired. Sore. Same with my legs.

Through the trees and out into the distance I could see
part of the day's journey. The valley was huge, that which
I could see in the light of dusk. It was a giant bowl. Maybe
I was on my way to climbing out of that bowl. The thought
made me excited and curious. Almost to the point where

I considered continuing on. To see what was on the other side. But I knew it was too far to go. I was already running on empty.

After using my hand spade to carve a level space the length and width of my body into the side of the mountain, sleep came and went just as I thought it would. Intervals. The night went on forever.

Late in the evening I saw light in the distance. Far away. A campfire. A lantern. Maybe a flashlight. It could've been anyone. It could've been my imagination. What was real and what wasn't was difficult to discern. And so I shut my eyes and went back to sleep. Not knowing.

When I was awake I thought about Sarah and I cried like a baby. I thought about Erin and the tears kept coming. I cried for her and what I had gotten us into. It was an unbelievably painful feeling to not be able to be with her. To protect her. A helpless feeling left me sick to my stomach. I just wanted to tell her everything. To say how sorry I was for lying. To tell her how much I loved her and what a mistake I had made. I looked up for a patch of sky. I saw a star in the distant night and began to pray. A conversation with God. A God whose church I hadn't stepped into for years. It went on for some time. Lying there on my side. Listening. Watching down below. Periodically turning my head and looking up between the branches and finding that star in heaven.

CHAPTER THIRTY-TWO

In my sleeping bag I watched the coming day make its arrival from its infancy. Daylight is a miracle. I rose with the sun like all diurnal life. Stood up and urinated on the trunk of a tree. Steam rising. It was colder than the morning before, and I put on the last of my wool long-sleeve shirts. Then I drank water and ate more trail mix. My food was running low, but it didn't concern me. The morning light conquered all. The new day. Amazing what it can do.

The climb up to the top of the hill took an hour. I paced myself. That was my goal for the day. Without knowing how far I would have to go, it was important to not overexert myself and burn out in a place that I didn't want to be. At the top I saw the new valley below and the old one behind me. I was traveling through a series of valleys that had the shape of elephant prints in wet mud. All connecting.

The view was worth the hike. I didn't care if anyone with the intent to bring harm could see me as I stood there at the top of my world. Above the tree line. A true Rocky Mountain high both physically and spiritually. There was such a sense of freedom as the wind came flowing up from the new valley and fluttered my clothing like it would a kite. The sun on my back making the cool breeze pleasant.

It was a good start to the morning. Admiring the million or so conifers down below. They covered the earth as far as I could see. But I saw a small area that they had missed. Like a brushstroke low on paint. It intrigued me. I took off my backpack and pulled out my binoculars. I saw a clearing with a structure on it. A cabin. I could just barely make it out, but it was a cabin or a barn. Life. It was the break I needed. I beamed with excitement and hope. For a few moments I kept looking at it. Playing with the focus to see if there was more to examine. Checking all surrounding areas for anything else. But there were only trees.

How I would make my way through the lower elevation once I was down there was my biggest concern. It was by no means a simple task. Being in and among the trees, I would have no way of getting a bearing on it. It would disappear. So I stood there thinking of a game plan. Eventually I figured that the cabin was most likely on or near a stream. The same stream I had been following and had planned to continue following. Connect with the water and let it deliver me home.

Down I went. There was nothing easy about it. No breaks. No yellow brick road. Blazing my way through some of the toughest terrain in the States. My mom's steadfast words ringing in my ears, "Come hell or high water." But I knew the water would eventually greet me, and it did.

It was so beautiful. So clear. Flowing downstream like a kiss good-bye. The gravel and rocks below the surface so polished and shiny in the sunlight. For a half mile or so I traveled along the bank. But it became difficult. The absence of any level terrain or obstacles made me dream of floating the river. With each step the temptation to just chuck it all and take my chances in the exposed water became more and more of a logical way to end my ordeal. It wasn't as though I was just giving up and throwing caution to the wind. I didn't feel that way. It was more along a line of thinking that what happened the last time I had taken the water route would not happen this time. My troubles were behind me and this was the quickest and easiest route to the cabin. To help.

So just like that I stopped in my tracks and scaled down the granite embankment and hit the water's edge. Ankle deep. It felt good. I took out my purifier and refilled my two bottles. I then began to look around for a log. The right log. There were plenty to choose from. I found two that were each about a yard long. I took the bungee cords that I had and lashed the logs together at each end. The raft was built. It would hold my backpack, and I attached it to it with the same bungee cords. Interconnecting it through the frame. Wrapping my sleeping bag in my poncho and stuffing it inside the pack. Hoping it might stay dry but not caring too much if it didn't. The finish line was near. Today was the day.

I journeyed down the river for a couple of hours and then could see an area up ahead that resembled what I had seen when I had spotted the cabin from above the tree line. I stopped. As much as I was in a hurry to reach this destination point, I also had to think about who might own the cabin. Contemplating the remoteness of the cabin, I wondered if it was owned by those who had taken Sarah and shot at me. Or maybe someone they were friends with. Or relatives. The world could be small. Feeling my heartbeat increasing, I pulled the raft out of the water. I would approach with caution. On land.

I had decided to approach the cabin area from high ground. Although I felt there was no real turning back at that point, that would at least give me the ability to check it out more thoroughly before fully committing to it. I hiked up a good ways, some of it very steep. It was tiring. Every so often I would stop. Catch my breath, look and listen, and then carry on. When I was high enough, I began paralleling the river. Not much longer I found a good spot that kept me hidden from view and yet allowed me to survey the cabin and surrounding clearing. I zeroed in with my binoculars, which I had dried off.

It was a rustic cabin. Logs were rough-hewn. One-story structure without a power line running to it. A black pipe stuck up through the roof. Two windows on either side of the front door, which was also made from logs or a log veneer. The windows were absent of curtains, and I tried to see anything inside. But there wasn't enough light to see. The front of the cabin wasn't in the direct path of the sun.

I felt myself becoming nervous. The place was primitive, and there were some similarities between it and the camp where Sarah had been held. There was a woodpile with chopped wood in the yard, and there were what appeared to be toys of some sort. Handcrafted from wood. Farther to the right of the house, a dirt road led off into the woods. Beyond the house was the stream, but I couldn't see it. I could only see the opposite bank, which was all rock. Another little canyon area I presumed, and the cabin sat near the edge. That was the reason for the clearing, as well as the trees that had been cut down for the cabin.

As committed as I had been earlier to the thought that this place would be my salvation, I found myself becoming more and more reluctant to go any farther. Hesitant. But that wasn't necessarily a bad thing to be. *Only fools rush in*, I told myself. *Patience is a virtue*, was another thought that ran through my mind. So I sat there hidden behind a tree, lying on my stomach on the ground, and waited and watched like a sniper without a gun. My wet shorts sticking to the dirt. Binoculars scanning everything around. When I put the binoculars down to have a look with the naked eye, I saw smoke coming out of the black pipe. Someone was in the cabin. I never could've imagined how the sight of smoke could have such an impact on me. Hope and fear, life or death. I stayed put, not knowing which one it was.

Ten minutes later the front door opened, and a balding, older man came out. He was wearing wire-rimmed glasses and had on a red-and-black flannel shirt and a pair of jeans that were tucked into his untied duck boots. I liked him right away. He reminded me of my dad. But still I didn't move. Observing. He picked up a couple of pieces of wood from the woodpile and then went back inside. A moment later he came back out and walked over to the road that faded into the trees. I heard a car door shut. It echoed across the canyon and up the hill I was on. He came back into view and was carrying a newspaper and a wicker fishing creel. My spirits were raised. Tremendously. It was hard to stay put. Surely I had seen enough. This man was not harmful. This man was my savior.

CHAPTER THIRTY-THREE

The first step up to the cabin door creaked loudly when my full weight set upon it. My presence was known. I knocked on the door with two quick taps and nervously waited. I heard him coming, and then the squeaky pine door opened.

"Hello, sir," I said as I looked him in the eye. Him looking at the ragged kid a third his age standing in his doorway with a tattered appearance and a beaten-down backpack. "I'm lost and could use some help." It was the truth.

I could see the uncertainty on his face, but I could also see what I thought was sympathy behind those glasses. "Come in." That was all he said. Expressionless like the smoke, and it didn't sit well with me. My heart, loud again.

The door swung open wide, and he led me into his cabin. It was one big room with a built-in wooden ladder leading up to a loft. The wood stove with exhaust pipe was in the center of the left wall. There was a pine table with two pine chairs next to some counters that appeared to be part of the kitchen area, and there were two sofas made from the same wood as the tables with thin cushions on them and folded-up wool blankets. All around were books, magazines, and newspapers. Several lanterns and candles sat on the end tables and the coffee table in between the two sofas. In one of the corners he kept his fishing gear. Rods and reels. In another corner he kept some tools for maintenance. On a wall hung a framed black-and-white photo of the *Spirit of Saint Louis.* When I saw that plane I knew I was in a good place.

We sat down across from each other on the sofas and he asked if I was thirsty. I didn't hesitate to accept his offer and he got up and went over toward the table and two chairs, and just below the counter that was next to them was an old metallic cooler. He opened it, and I heard the ice shifting as he reached in for the can.

He brought back an ice-cold Pepsi.

"Here you go, and I've got another one too if you want it."

"Thanks."

I opened it and took a big sip. I had never tasted anything so good. It was gone in seconds. He was smiling. Amused at my enjoyment of such a simple thing. And then I burped loudly. Couldn't help it.

"So tell me what's happened to you." He was curious, as anyone would be. "And by the way, my name is Warren."

"I'm Alex. Alex Cavanaugh." I put the empty can on the table. I wanted the second one but didn't ask. Thought it was better to wait until he offered again.

"Warren Piersma," he said as he reached over and we shook hands. "Nice to meet you."

There was a pipe on the end table next to him. He picked it up, and the matches next to it.

"Thank you so much, Mr. Piersma, for—"

"Please, call me Warren." He struck the match to light his briarwood pipe.

"OK, Warren. Well thank you so much for letting me intrude on you like this." He just kept puffing on his pipe to get it lit. "I left two days ago to hike in to Oar Lake to do some fishing, and somehow I got lost. I have no idea where I am." Kept it short and sweet.

"I'm not familiar with Oar Lake. Where did you hike in from?"

"I live in Aspen, and a friend of mine dropped me off at the Mineral King trailhead a few miles out of town."

"Well you've certainly come a long way."

He leaned forward toward the coffee table and shuffled through some books and magazines until he found what he was looking for. It was a map printed by the National Forest Service. When unfolded, it covered the entire table.

"Look here," he said to me, and I leaned forward. He turned the map so that I could read it, his finger staying in the same position. "This is where we are. That's Bear Creek out back, and it connects into Taylor Creek, which runs to Taylor Reservoir. Somewhere along the way you crossed over the Continental Divide, and you're now as close to Crested Butte, where I live, as you are to Aspen. You sure have traveled far."

I couldn't believe where I was. I looked back down at the map and seared it into my mind. Memorizing it like the phone number Erin gave me the day we met. Marking the location of his cabin and the likely route I took to get there. The proximity of it to the cocaine that I had hidden and would have to retrieve. I saw Aspen clearly marked in the center, and I saw Erin staring right back at me. Then Sarah.

"I can't believe how far off course I am. Do you think you could drop me off in town so I could have my girl-friend pick me up there?" He didn't say a thing at first. Just puffed on the pipe. Eyeing me over. Probably knew there was much more to my story than what I'd given him. It seemed like an eternity but finally he said, "No problem. You just tell me when you want to leave."

"I'm ready to go whenever you are."

He stood up. "Alright, how about if we take a few things to eat and drink for the ride? You have to be hungry, and I saw how much you liked that Pepsi."

"Sure, that would be great," I said. "I can't thank you enough, Warren. You're a lifesaver."

"I wouldn't say that. You seem to be a pretty resourceful. I'm sure you would've just kept on walking all the way to Crested Butte or Gunnison had you not found me."

He put some apples, hard salami, and canned peanuts in his fishing creel, which functioned as his small pack, and then he told me to grab a few drinks out of the cooler for us. I took another Pepsi and a couple of 7UPs. I followed him out of the cabin and past the woodpile to where his beige Suburban was parked. The back of the Suburban was loaded up with all kinds of tools and gear, and I saw pieces of wood just like on his furniture and realized that he had probably made all of it. We got in, and he started it up. Made a circle in the clearing, and then we headed down the road. His driveway.

"We've got a bit of a ride, and the road isn't very good, so we have to take it kind of slow," he said. "Hope you don't mind the bumps."

"I don't mind at all."

The Suburban bumped and bounced like Jell-O, but it had a kind of soothing effect. A rhythm to it. My eyes wanted to shut, but I fought it. It was too important to remember everything so that I could return. Each time I felt my head falling down, I'd yank it back up and strike up a conversation. Anything to stay awake.

"If you want to shut your eyes and take a nap go right ahead," he said, my fatigue so obvious.

"I'm OK. I think it's just that the seat feels so nice, and I haven't been this comfortable in a few days. I really don't want to sleep." God how that seat felt so good.

"Well you're more than welcome to if you'd like."

"Thanks, I appreciate that."

After about a mile we turned out of his drive and onto the main dirt road. I noted the little totem pole that marked the entrance to his drive. It was a good landmark.

I learned that he had built the cabin himself and made all the furniture as well. He purchased the wood from a special lumberyard in Telluride, where he said he would be driving to early in the morning. Working with wood was his hobby. It kept him busy now that he was retired from General Electric, where he had worked thirty-seven years. He'd held several management positions within the company and had been transferred around the country with each of them. It was difficult uprooting the family with each move, but that was part of life when working for one of the world's largest companies he said. To offset the changes, he and his wife always took the kids on their annual ski trip to Crested Butte. They all loved the little town. It had become their favorite place to visit, and it was where they vacationed every winter, and then eventually every summer too. He and his wife agreed that one day they would retire there. The kids would come visit. Ski in the winter and enjoy the mountains in the summer. So they bought the land on Bear Creek first. It was an opportunity they couldn't pass up. A friend of a friend of a friend sort of thing. They had no intention of building a home there. It would just be a piece of land to play with. Not long after that purchase, they bought a home in town.

At some point during the ride, I nodded off. When I awoke, we were still on 317 and nearing Emerald Lake. With each slow-going mile I grew more and more excited to see Erin. But I also knew that I had turned our lives upside down, and there were so many problems that we were going to have to deal with right away. Warren had offered to take me all the way to Aspen, but I insisted that Carbondale was far enough. I would have him drop me off at the gas station, and I would use the phone there. My first call had to be to Carter to straighten things out, and then I would call Erin. She would come get me. I would tell her everything, and then we would plan our next step. This would be better than just showing up on our doorstep. For some reason I knew that going directly home was not the right thing to do. A gut feeling.

The Suburban pulled into Carbondale and then turned into the gas station. It had been a long ride. The two of us got out, and he reached into the back to get my pack.

"That's OK, I can get it," I said.

"How about at least letting me give you a dollar so you can get change for the phone," he said. I had thought about making collect calls, but it made sense to take him up on his offer to make things easier.

"Actually, that would be great."

He took out his wallet, grabbed a bill, folded it up, and stuck it in my hand. "Good luck, Alex."

"Thank you so much, Warren. You have no idea how much this means to me. Someday I hope I get the chance to return the favor."

"No problem. It's been a pleasure to help."

We shook hands, and he got in his car and drove away. The back of his hand sticking out the driver's side window and waving to me.

CHAPTER THIRTY-FOUR

The pay phone was outside over by the air hose. I walked into the station and pulled out the money and asked the attendant for two quarters and five dimes. She looked at me funny. When I looked down at the bill I saw it was a twenty. Warren Piersma's kindness overwhelmed me.

She changed the twenty, and then I went back outside, carrying my backpack with my right arm, and walked over to the pay phone. I dialed Carter's number. The late-afternoon sun forcing me to turn and face the pumps. It rang and rang. Finally he picked up.

"Carter, it's Alex."

"Alex, what the fuck is going on? We are both in some serious shit, my friend."

"I can explain everything," I told him, knowing that my story was going to be hard for him, or anyone, to believe.

"I sure hope you can. There are some very angry people who want some answers. And I think you know what I'm talking about."

He wasn't going to talk business or say anything that could incriminate himself over the phone. He was always smart enough to cover his bases. So I said nothing as well. "Have you talked to Erin?" I asked.

"I talked to her earlier this morning."

"Is she OK?"

"Where are you, Alex?"

"You didn't answer my question, Carter." The tension was mounting, and I knew both of us could feel it. So I thought it was best to defuse it. I was thinking of Erin. Of both of us. "I'm down in Carbondale."

"Where in Carbondale? I'll come get you."

"I'm at the gas station."

"OK, I'm on my way. Just wait for me there."

"Can you pick up Erin on the way?"

"That's probably not a good idea. You and I need to talk first."

"Carter, does she know about everything?"

"Yes, I had to fill her in. I didn't have a choice."

I paused and thought about how she probably reacted, the disappointment she must have felt. "OK, see you in a half hour."

As soon as I hung up, I put more coins in the phone and called our apartment. *Come on, Erin, answer the phone,*

I said to myself as it kept ringing. After many rings I hung up. The change came back out of the phone. I put it back in and dialed again. Thinking maybe I had dialed the wrong number. Again no answer. As a long shot I tried her work, but I knew that on a beautiful Sunday nobody would be there, including Erin. More change returned. Her best friend in town was Megan Singleton, but I didn't know her number. The operator found it for me. No answer there either. I tried another friend who did answer, but she hadn't seen or heard from Erin. My call had only worried her, so I simply said I had locked myself out of our apartment. Nothing important.

I went back into the gas station and bought a six-pack of Coors. Outside I found a shady spot, and opened one. Sitting on the sleeping bag all rolled up and strapped to the backpack. Cushion. The ice-cold beer incredibly perfect. If ever there could be such a thing. I would share the others with Carter on our ride back to Aspen. As I took another sip I saw the newspaper in its stand, and on the front page there was a picture of Sarah Evans. Reality came flooding back.

Carter's blue-and-white Blazer pulled into the station. I stood up. I could see in his eyes that he thought I looked like shit. Which I did. And that was a good thing. Add credibility to the story I would be telling him. He didn't look so good either. There was a roughness about him. Maybe it was his customary five o'clock shadow that looked five hours late and the trucker cap that looked completely out of place on his head. The plain white T-shirt that he was wearing threw me off as well.

He came to a stop, and I opened the back door and threw in my backpack. Then I climbed up into the front passenger seat. The newspaper rolled up in one hand and my beer in the other. The rest of the six pack cradled like a football.

"Let's just head up the road a few miles and we'll have a long talk," he said, not even looking at me as he put it in gear and we got on Highway 82 heading toward Aspen. I opened a beer and handed it to him. It was a good sign that he took it.

Not much was said between us. It would come out soon enough. After seven or eight miles, he turned off Highway 82 and onto a farm road near the junction of the Roaring Fork and Frying Pan rivers. The "No Hunting," "No Fishing," and "No Trespassing" signs were prominently posted to keep people out. We drove right by them like we owned the place. Obviously he had been there before and knew exactly where he was going. There was water up ahead. I could see the trees lining the banks. The Roaring Fork. Somewhere after its confluence with the Frying Pan. Though I had fished many sections of the river, I was in an area that I had never been before. This stretch was on private property, and these waters were fiercely protected by their owners. Keeping people like myself out.

We came to a stop at the end of the road. The river just beyond. We both got out and then walked over to a picnic table that had weathered many seasons. It was perpendicular to the water. We sat down across from each other.

The extra beers and newspaper between us. Within arm's reach. Looking to my right was one of the most beautiful stretches of the Roaring Fork that I had ever seen. And it was just as pretty to listen to as it was to watch.

I decided to break the ice. "Whose place is this?"

"A friend of mine," was all he said. Never looking at me. His beer cupped between both hands on the table. The sun getting lower on the horizon and being filtered by the tree branches. Hitting our sides without its full strength.

The awkwardness of the silence forced me to reach for another beer and open it.

"Have you fished this stretch?" I asked. A second attempt to move things forward.

"I haven't," he replied. He looked me in the eye. "Where's the coke, Alex?"

"It's up in the mountains where I hid it. It's in a safe place," I told him. He glanced away at the river and then back to me. "And before you jump to conclusions, as anyone would, let me explain that I am the only person in the world who knows what happened to this girl." I picked up the front page of the *Denver Post* and showed him Sarah's picture. His face remained expressionless. "And I'm the only guy who knows where the coke is," I finished, reinforcing the fact that if something happened to me, then $2 million of blow would be lost forever. There had to be a reason why he had taken me to a remote location, so I began raising my defenses.

He took a sip of his beer and then put his Ray-Ban aviator sunglasses on. My reflection creating a small picture in the left lens.

"Why don't you just start from the beginning?"

"That's what I want to do, and I'm going to tell you everything. And it's all true. As unbelievable as some of it's going to sound to you," I replied. I could see his eyes from behind his sunglasses glance down at his watch. It put some thoughts in my head. Negative ones.

"I'm all ears," he said as though he was certain my story was going to be nothing but bullshit and the two of us were wasting each other's time.

Whether or not I had his full attention, I began telling him of my ordeal over the last few days. He sat and listened. I went into detail on everything. Proof that something like this could not be made up. Dreamed up. I got up, went over to his Blazer, grabbed my backpack, walked back and pulled out Sarah's running shorts. I knew then that I definitely had his attention. He touched them. The fabric running between his fingers. His sunglasses came off for a closer inspection. The temple tip resting on his lower lip. I didn't say a word. Just let him take it all in. The ConAgra logo on the running shorts. The sunglasses returned to his eyes.

"I'm listening," was all he said.

I resumed with my story. Remembering everything as best I could. Showing him where the bullet had hit the backpack. The wound on my back. The remainder of the money that Warren had given me. When I finished, he opened a beer and handed it to me. I took it as a sign that he finally believed me.

"Sounds like you've been through hell," he said as he picked up a little stone and tossed it into the river.

"I have been," I replied. "And I'm telling you the truth. I would never screw you over."

He turned back around from the river and brought his leg up onto the bench seat. Leaning forward with his arms folded across his knee.

"There are some angry people who want their coke, Alex, and we have to get it to them. This is some serious shit we've gotten ourselves in."

"I need to get to Erin," I said, making it as clear as possible that she was my first concern.

"The best thing you can do for her is to get the coke you've hidden and bring it to me."

"I can do that. And I've known all along that I would have to go back up there and get it," I told him. "But I have to see Erin first. And I need to rest for a night or two. I hope you can understand this."

"I understand, but there are some people who don't, and they don't care about you or anything that's happened to you. I'm just telling you the way it is. They won't hesitate to hurt you, or me, if they think they've been screwed," he said as he turned back toward the river. "This business is not for the faint of heart." It came across like he was questioning his own involvement as much as mine. "You can't go home. They're waiting for you there. That's why I brought you here."

Though I still had doubts, I was relieved to know that it seemed like he was looking out for me and not setting me up. But all I could think about was Erin. "Then we need to find Erin right now. She isn't safe either, is she? Tell me the truth, Carter."

He paused for a moment. Took a sip of his beer and then put it down on the tabletop.

"I talked to her this morning after she drove to the airport."

"Aspen airport?" He could see I'd become agitated. "Why didn't you tell me this earlier?"

"Listen to me," he began, "I had no idea where you were or what was going on. For all I knew you were in Hawaii with two million dollars' worth of coke I entrusted you with and Erin was on her way to meet you there. Slipping out of town and never coming back."

"What airport?" I asked again.

"Aspen."

"Why was she there?"

"I don't know why she was there. Usually people go to the airport to fly somewhere, right?" I didn't reply. I knew what he was getting at. "I told her to stay inside your apartment until we got this thing cleared up. But she left and drove to the airport, and then she went back home. I'm not sure if she's still there though."

"How do you know all this?"

"Because there are people following her, and they've called me a few times to let me know what's going on."

"Are you with them or us?"

"I just want the coke returned to its rightful owners. That solves everything, and we all walk away."

It wasn't the answer I wanted to hear, but I felt at least it was honest, and for the time being that was good enough for me. There had to be some sort of trust established. Even if it was based on reaching a mutually beneficial dissolution of our business arrangement. We would go our separate ways. Put things back in order and not even worry about time healing old wounds. It would never be talked about. Gently swept under the table. That is how he and I would handle it. But there was a third party, and they just wanted their coke. The sooner the better.

When he drove away, I opened the last can of beer and walked over to the grove of trees that lined the river bank. The trunk of a tree to lean up against. The shade. The water, the mountains, and the sky to look at. What a perfect place to cast a fly. The undercut bank across from me. Surely a holding place for a large rainbow trout. Thoughts to take my mind off Erin. Even if it was for just a moment.

I had confidence in Carter finding Erin. It seemed as though she wasn't out of eyesight and he'd be able to convince his business partners that she needed to go with him as part of his plan to find me. They wouldn't be aware of us having already met up. We came to the conclusion they would never believe my story, so we decided to not even try to sell it. It was best to keep me in the shadows. I would remain where I was. Meet with Erin. Hug and kiss her. Make certain she was safe. Patch things up if needed, which I was certain there was the need. Then I would head back into the mountains in the morning. Carter would bring me fresh supplies, including a sidearm. I wasn't going back through hell without a gun. He would take me as far as Warren's cabin, and I would follow the river. Look for the landmarks. I would remember them. I would find the coke. I could do it in a day. My reward would be Erin waiting for me, coupled with the ability to seek justice for Sarah and her family by doing what I could in ridding her butchers from society. The future was hopeful. I saw the summit of Everest, not the false one, and would soon be reaching it. One more day.

I became so tired laying there under those trees. Eventually I couldn't even move an inch. I was as spent as the empty beer can in my right hand, and I fell asleep. Too exhausted to dream.

CHAPTER THIRTY-FIVE

When I awoke, it was dark. In the shape of an Allen wrench, I was leaning against the tree, my backpack right next to me. The beer can lay on the ground by my hand. I looked at my watch and saw that it was nine forty-five. Carter had been gone several hours and should've returned. With Erin. Something wasn't right, and disappointment and sobriety settled in. Without a car there wasn't much I could do, and if Carter and Erin were on their way and I wasn't here when they arrived, then leaving and searching for them would be a big mistake. I struggled with the idea of doing nothing and waiting. I had always been better on the move. Taking action. To a fault to some degree. Just to kill time I flipped the backpack on my back and buckled it. Then took it off. Then back on. Like saddling up a horse. I was ready to go. Anywhere. Anywhere Erin was.

Midnight was the deadline. I wouldn't wait around a minute longer. That was the deal I made with myself. So when it came, and still no arrival, I rounded up the empty beer cans—attempting to be somewhat of a good steward of the land—and put them on the table next to Sarah's shorts. Then I began my trek back to Highway 82. With luck, I could hitch a ride to El Jebel or Basalt, or maybe even Aspen. Someone on their way to their night shift, or on their way to a bar or returning from one.

It took thirty minutes to make it to the highway. When I got there I was disappointed to see how deserted it was. A ride was not going to come easy. Darkness was my other problem. I was only visible at close range. That would only encourage drivers to keep going, keep their momentum, rather than stopping when seeing me at the last second. So I took out my flashlight to shine it on myself when I saw headlights approaching. I waited. With my backpack on. It made me look more like a hiker than a vagabond. Less threatening, if there could be such a thing on the side of an empty road at midnight. Finally some lights. Heading in my direction. My outstretched arm with my thumb up. The flashlight illuminating my haggard appearance. As it approached its high beams flicked on. Blinding me. And then it sped by. A station wagon. Another car then came from the other direction.

It wasn't going my way, so I didn't pay any attention to it. Kept my eyes looking for the cars that had potential. When I could hear it slowing down, I turned around to check it out. The cruiser then turned on its flashing lights and made a U-turn. When the floodlight by the driver's window lit me up, my heart sank. The cruiser came to a rest on the berm right in front of me. The Colorado Highway Patrol. Written there on the passenger door. I had to lean to the left to get out of the lights to read it. The floodlight following me.

A moment later the trooper emerged from his car. Wide-brimmed hat finding its place on his head. Shirt and pants full of starch. Slowly he made his way to me. I could see he was at least sixty years old, though sturdy for his age. An inch or two shorter than my six-foot-one-inch frame. His sideburns were white and gray. Unlike his uniform, he had a face full of wrinkles from years of exposure to the Colorado sun. When he turned slightly to the right, I caught the name Dearman on the silver nameplate pinned to his chest.

"What are you doing out here in the middle of the night?" he asked, putting his hands on each side of his utility belt that wrapped around his waist. Never far from his sidearm.

"I'm trying to make it home, sir." I was as polite and respectful as I could be.

"Where might that be?"

"Aspen."

"How did you end up here?" The interrogation continued.

"I was hiking up in the mountains and got lost." Same line I'd given Warren Piersma.

He took his flashlight out of his belt and shone it on me. The car lights and flood were still on as well. He shone it right in my eyes and moved in closer.

"Have you been drinking?"

"I had a few beers that I bought down in Carbondale earlier, but that was hours ago."

He got close enough to smell my breath. A mouth that hadn't seen a toothbrush and toothpaste for days. He then leaned back. I wasn't sure what he was looking for or what crime I had possibly committed by being there on the side of the highway trying to hitch a ride to Aspen. With or without alcohol in my system. Then I began thinking that maybe the police were looking for me. Maybe Erin had gone to the police. Or maybe this was one of the patrols that Carter had become so worried about, thus creating his courier service that I had signed on to.

"What's your name?"

"Alex Cavanaugh."

"Do you have any ID on you, Alex?"

"I don't, Officer. My wallet is at home. I took a few dollars with me when I left to go hiking, but that's it other than what I have in my backpack."

"We'll get to that in a moment. I'm going to ask you to step into the back of the cruiser for a moment, Alex."

"Why? What have I done wrong, sir?" I was somewhat alarmed at being asked to have my freedom taken away and being forced to sit in the back of his cruiser where the door handles are on the outside.

"If you'll just take off your backpack and lean it up against the car." He motioned for me to lean it up against the front right fender. He then went and opened the back door to the cruiser for me. "Please have a seat, Alex."

I did as he asked, knowing it was better to cooperate and be polite and respectful. I had remembered watching two of my friends get thrown into a paddy wagon my junior year in college when they mouthed off and refused to obey the cops who had come to shut down a late-night party. He put his hand on the top of my head as I lowered myself into the car.

"Would you mind if I took a look inside your backpack?" he asked.

"No, not at all."

He took the flashlight back out of his belt again and inspected the outside of my pack. Then he opened up the external pockets. Rummaging through each one. He uncoiled the bungee cord and unraveled my sleeping bag and pad. Nothing. He rolled it back nicely and reattached it to my pack. Lastly he opened up the main pocket that days prior had been filled with coke. He pulled out some of my clothes. Rummaged through them. Stuffed them back in. He walked around to the driver's side door and got into the driver's seat. I remained silent in the back, wondering if he had become suspicious of the emptiness of the pack.

"Alex, what is your social security number and address?" he asked as he prepared to write down my information on a piece of paper attached to a clipboard. He was all business. Direct, but professional.

I gave him the information he wanted, and then he picked up the microphone for his police radio. He got a dispatcher and gave her my information. I knew he was just checking my background. Making sure I was who I said I was. She also came back with a negative on warrants, which cleared me completely. I would be free to go. But that wasn't necessarily a good option either. I would just be back on the highway. So I turned the tables a little in my favor.

"Officer, can I ask you for a favor?"

"I'll do what I can," he replied as he finished up some paperwork and began to reach for his hat to exit the car and come around to let me out.

"Would you mind giving me a lift to Basalt so that I can call my girlfriend to come pick me up?"

"Unfortunately, it's against regulations to transport citizens for travel purposes, and I'm not headed in that direction. We're in the middle of a homicide investigation that occurred a short while ago in Aspen, and I'm patrolling the highway from there to Glenwood Springs." My heart stopped as he grabbed his hat and keys. "I can take you to Glenwood Springs and drop you off there."

"What happened in Aspen?" I was hoping that Sarah's body had been found, and the police were in hot pursuit of the animals who killed her and shot me.

"White male, thirty-five years old, was found with gunshot wounds in the head and chest. He was shot in his vehicle. Carter Pate. Ever heard of him?" he asked, knowing that Aspen was a small town.

"No, I just moved there a couple months ago." The words did not come out easily and I wondered if he could tell that I was lying. I passed.

"Thought I'd ask. Would you like me to let you out here or in Glenwood? It's awfully dangerous to be on this highway at night, and I highly advise you going with me."

"OK, sure, I'll head with you to Glenwood," I told him, trying my best to be as normal sounding as possible, though I could feel every muscle in my body tightening and the knot growing in my stomach.

It was painful to be headed in the opposite direction of Erin, but I wanted to get to a phone as fast as possible. It would be the quickest way to find her. The news of Carter was shocking. My hands were shaking, and I slid them under my ass in an attempt to calm them down and keep them hidden. As much as I wanted to be out of that cruiser and away from that cop, I had to make it to a phone as quickly as possible, and he was my fastest way there.

He got back out of the car and went and picked up my backpack. Opened up the back door and handed it to me.

Then off we went. A mile down the road the dispatcher came over the radio: "Suspect, male, Caucasian, early forties, black Camaro, Colorado plates." There were some other things, but I didn't understand the police jargon.

"What's going on, Officer?"

"They're putting out an APB of the suspect in the shooting. Looks like there was a witness. We know it's drug related. Always is, even in our little Colorado towns," he replied, sounding somewhat defeated.

He then got back on the radio indicating his position and his approximate time of arrival in Glenwood. His eyes scanning the oncoming car. I wanted to ask more questions, but the more I spoke the more chance I had of saying something I shouldn't.

There was nothing open in Glenwood but the Exxon station and a few bars. I could tell he didn't feel comfortable letting me off at either one.

"Why don't I drop you at the Hotel Colorado. I think you'll have more options there," he said. It was a big hotel that was a local landmark for its hot springs pool. Famous visitors. An ex-president or two having dipped into the waters there. It was somewhat familiar to me and sounded like a good spot. "They might not like the way you look, but I certainly don't think they will bar you from their doors."

"That sounds good, sir. I appreciate it."

We made our way down through the center of town, and at the end where I-70 cut through the western edge of Glenwood Canyon, the hotel sat prominently overlooking Glenwood Springs. He pulled into the parking lot, put the car in park, and then the same routine of keys, hat, and exit. He came around and opened my door. We shook hands, and I thanked him for the ride.

"Our secret," he said.

"It's safe with me."

He got back in and drove away. The night air felt cooler, and I reached in my pack for my parka. It would also dress me up a bit. An upscale hotel. Nice clientele. The staff would be more likely to help if I looked more like someone of means than the midnight hiker that I was. The lobby was empty. Just a clerk at the front desk. She was cute. In her uniform. Her summer college job. She looked at me and didn't show any hint of looking down upon me. It was good that we were close in age. A common bond. I walked over to her but stood back from the counter a foot or two. I knew I had to smell.

"Good evening, how may I help you?" she said with a smile. Her braided ponytail peeking out from her back just below her left shoulder.

"I'm doing OK. A little tired," I replied. She remained smiling. "I was wondering if I could use your phone to make a call." I tried my best to be as charming as possible.

"There's a pay phone just past the lobby at the bottom of the steps on the lower level," she replied, pointing the way.

Quickly I walked to the lower level and found the phone. Just down the hall from the hotel bar. I had change in my pocket, but it was easier to just make collect calls. I called our apartment. No answer. Then I had the operator locate Megan Singleton's number again, and she connected me to it. On the second ring Megan picked up. Felt my luck changing. She accepted the charges from the operator.

"Megan, it's Alex."

"Oh my God, Alex, Erin has been looking all over for you."

"And I've been looking for her. Is she there? I need to talk to her."

"She was earlier, but then she left. She's coming back though. Where are you?"

"I'm down in Glenwood Springs. What time is she coming back, and where'd she go?"

"She should be back soon. She said she had to get something from your apartment."

"How long ago was that?"

"About an hour ago. Did you hear about Carter?"

"I did. I still can't believe it." More lies.

"It's all over the news, and everyone is freaked out about it. Erin is a mess, Alex. She is so upset about it."

"Listen, Megan, I'm going to call over to the apartment, and while I'm doing that if Erin shows up tell her not to go anywhere. Do you have a pen and paper?"

"Hang on a sec," she replied. She put the phone down, and I could hear her looking. She came back to the phone. "OK, I'm ready."

I gave her the number to the pay phone and told her again to not let Erin go anywhere if she showed up, and if she needed me for anything to call me right away. I would be back in touch in a few minutes. I hung up and then had the operator make another collect call to our apartment. The phone rang and rang and rang, and all the while I was saying to myself, *Come on, Erin, pick up the phone.* She never did. I had hoped she was on her way to Megan's, or even walking through her door.

I hung up and called Megan back, collect. She answered right away. Still no Erin. My stomach shrinking. Fear. Anxiety. Helplessness. Stranded in Glenwood. All I wanted was to protect Erin, and yet I could do nothing of the sort. I told Megan that I was going to wait another fifteen minutes for Erin to arrive at her place. She was to call me right away if she showed up. When the fifteen minutes was up and if she still didn't arrive, then Megan was to call me and then come down to Glenwood Springs and pick me up. Leaving a note on her door telling Erin that she would be back by one thirty in the morning and to come inside and wait for her. That she had spoken to me. She would also leave the number of the pay phone that I was using and would wait by.

The minutes seemed like days, and after fifteen the phone rang and I picked it up. No Erin. Megan was on her way. I called our apartment collect every two minutes while I waited for Megan. It was all I could do. I ran things through my mind, and I couldn't figure out where she would be if she wasn't at home or at Megan's, unless something had happened to her. Forty-five minutes into the wait the pay phone rang and my name was the first word she spoke. A voice more beautiful than her eyes.

"Erin, tell me you're OK." It's all I wanted to know.

I never knew you could shed tears of joy, sorrow and guilt at the same time, but I proved it to be true. She was safe and unharmed, and that created the flood. But Sarah wasn't, and her body remained up in the mountains—cold and alone, and still missing. The flood breached the dam, and all of the other emotions and anxiety that had weighed so heavily upon me for days sustained the torrent.

"I've been so worried about you," she said, and broke down.

Neither of us spoke until we regained our composure. "Me too. Everything is going to be OK. Megan is coming to get me, and then we'll be back at her place in no time, and I'm never going to let you out of my sight again." She made me promise that it would come true.

"Carter told me everything," She then said. I could hear the disappointment as easily as I had heard the tears.

"I have so much to tell you, Erin. I am so sorry for all of this. I love you more than you will ever know."

"I love you too."

She had begun to tell me that Megan only knew that I had gone hiking to a lake to fish and hadn't returned on time, thus the worry, and that she'd been driving around looking for me, and then I saw Megan coming down the hotel steps. It was so hard to say good-bye to her. To give up that phone. To give up her voice.

"We're on our way. Lock the door and don't open it for anyone other than Megan and me. We'll be there in forty-five minutes."

The road was empty. But a late-night drive on Highway 82 meant deer. We had to go slow. I did my best to keep things short and simple with Megan. I had the feeling she knew there was more going on than Erin and I had told her. And the coincidence of Carter's death just didn't add up. But she didn't press me. Easy to see why she and Erin were close. I mostly looked out the window into the dark night thinking of what was to come. The radio on.

Just beyond Basalt there was a Pitkin County Sheriff cruiser hidden off the side of the road. Lights out. A likely spot to nab speeders and DUI offenders. But I also knew from the state trooper that they were heavily patrolling the area surrounding Aspen. Looking for the suspect in Carter's death. We went driving by. Memories of Carter traveling with me.

Megan's house was in Snowmass, a ski area a few miles down the road from Aspen. It was her parents' place, but they only visited from time to time. A few times a year. Both were lawyers in the music industry, which kept them mostly in Los Angeles. And LA was the connection that attached Erin and Megan when they first met each other. As soon as the two of them found out they shared the same hometown they became instant friends. And it grew from there.

The house was high up on the mountain at the end of a long, unlit, private drive. Designed that way for privacy. It was a modest home for Snowmass. The old A-frame that had once stood on the property had been torn down and replaced with a modern four-bedroom glass-and-stone structure. Plenty of ceiling-to-floor windows so that the surrounding mountains were never out of sight during the daylight hours. There was a two-car attached garage with plenty of storage for skis and the two snowmobiles that Megan had promised we would be riding come winter.

Erin's car parked in the driveway was a welcome sight. Megan clicked the garage door opener, and eased the car into her space in the garage. Right away the door to the house opened, and Erin came out in her faded Levi's, boots, and white V-neck T-shirt with "Hotel Jerome" in small print on her chest. Beautiful as ever. I held her tight. No words. Just held her.

"I'm sure you two want to be alone, so I'm going to go on inside," Megan said, and she left Erin and me alone in the garage.

After a few minutes of just holding her and kissing her, I wiped away her tears and leaned back against the front of Megan's warm car with Erin in between my legs. We looked each other in the eyes. Her amazing eyes.

"I've been through hell and back, and I just want you to listen to me, OK," I said, and I started at the beginning.

From the moment Carter asked me to courier the coke for him. The first trip in June. How everything went so well. How I got the money to buy her the new cowboy boots and bracelet that I showed up with at home one day. And then the second time. How I lost my way. Found Sarah, and everything that followed.

CHAPTER THIRTY-SIX

"We have to contact the police." It was the first thing out of Erin's mouth when I finished telling her everything.

"I know we do, and I know you're really scared and so am I. But we can't do it yet. Carter's business partners want their two million dollars' worth of coke, and they will go to any length to get it. Taking care of them is my first priority because that's the only way I can keep you safe. Then we can help Sarah and her family."

"Not even after seeing what happened to Carter?"

I shook my head in disagreement, and replied, "I know what needs to be done."

She just kept looking up at me. I prodded her to tell me what she was thinking. "I didn't tell you this before because

I didn't want to worry you when you were down in Glenwood, but there were two guys following me today, and I think they have something to do with Carter's death," she said with a concerned look on her face. "They were watching me to get to you."

"Carter told me about them. Listen to me, Erin, they just want their coke back, and I'm the only one who knows where it is. So they aren't going to do anything that would jeopardize that."

She took a deep breath and slowly let it out. "This is all so messed up."

"It is, and it's my fault. But I know how to fix it."

"You're going back up there, aren't you?" she said with the saddest look in her eyes. The thought of us separating again lowered her spirits and mine.

I put my arms around her and then brushed her hair behind the ears. "I have to. These guys who are involved with Carter are not people we want anything to do with. I made a big mistake. But I know how to correct it."

I was going to have to go back up into the mountains and retrieve the coke, give it to its rightful owners, and then wash my hands of any involvement. Be done with it. Then and only then could I help Sarah and her family. The sooner the better. Closure for those in the dark, and bars for the ones responsible for shutting the curtains on them. But I was exhausted and needed to rest before continuing.

Megan's was not a safe place to stay. Whether or not Erin had been able to lose her trackers at the airport,

Megan would be on anyone's checklist, and Carter had made it clear who we were dealing with. I had decided we would go to Warren Piersma's cabin. She would stay there while I made the trek. It was safe. Unknown to anyone we knew. And nobody would be able to follow us without our noticing, especially the last twenty miles of that mountain road.

We went back inside and thanked Megan. Told her we were going home. Getting a good night's sleep. Just happy to be back together. All of us agreed to inform one another of any developments in Carter's death, and then we said our good-byes.

She closed the garage door behind us and then turned off the outside lights. At the top of that mountain we were deep into the night. You could feel it like loneliness. Erin tossed me the keys to her Jeep. The two of us got in, and I turned it around to head down the long, winding driveway. I was not looking forward to the drive back out to the cabin. It was a strenuous undertaking at that time of night, especially with the limited sleep she and I were working off of. Most likely we would find a secluded place along the way to pull over and shut our eyes. There was also no hurry to get to the cabin early. I wanted to make sure that Warren was long on his way to Telluride. I flipped on the high beams. They were necessary. With each turn though the white bark of the aspens was as blinding as mountain snow in sunlight. Forcing me to flip them off. Then back on again as we came out of the turn. On and off, in and out of the turns. Slowly meandering our way down the mountain like beginners on skis.

Suddenly, as we came out of a turn, a parked car facing us in the middle of the road flipped on its high beams. From complete darkness, two powerful front headlights shone into our windshield. Far more powerful than the reflections on the aspens. I slammed on the brakes, coming to a quick stop and narrowly avoiding a head-on collision. Erin didn't have on her seat belt and almost hit her forehead on the windshield. Her arms outstretched onto the dashboard, stopping the impact at the last second. I kept myself upright with my hands on the steering wheel. Just my head thrusting forward.

Three men came flying out of the silver-colored four-door Mercedes. Guns drawn. It happened so fast. They came upon both sides of our jeep. I could do nothing. Erin started screaming and crouched her head down below her window and brought her knees up to her chest. Full tuck position. I waited for the bullets to hit us. Hands still on the wheel. I wasn't even breathing. They threw open our doors. I reached over for Erin to protect her. What little I could do. Put my body over hers. Everything happening so quickly that I acted by instinct alone.

"Get out now," the big, bald-headed man on my side of the Jeep shouted at us. His nine millimeter pistol was aimed right at my head. He was well over six feet and muscular in his jeans and black army boots. An intimidating forty-something-year-old man with a goatee the same color as the boots and cotton sweater he wore with the sleeves pulled up. Tattoos on both forearms.

I sat up and raised my hands. Showing that they were empty. Unarmed. I looked him in the eyes to let him know that I was going to do what he said. Erin kept crouching, and the guy on her side reached in to grab hold of her arm. I leaned toward him, not liking him touching Erin, and he shoved his pistol right up against my head. It stopped me in my tracks. Unlike the Caucasian on my side of the car, he was Latino. Smaller in build, yet every bit as frightening in his all-black attire and wielding a firearm. His eyes were blank. As cold as the steel barrel of the gun resting against my right temple.

"Erin, we have to get out of the car," I said, not moving an inch of my body.

She was crying, and I needed to calm her down. The third guy stood at the front of the Jeep and was pointing his pistol right at us too. His feet shoulder width apart. Center of gravity forward. Arms out in a combat stance. Never taking us out of his sight. Hardened Eastern European, or maybe Argentinean. The youngest of the three. Jet-black hair pulled back into a short ponytail. A short-sleeve gray polo shirt showcasing his biceps hung out over his khaki pants with cargo pockets. With military speed and precision, they had us at their mercy.

"I'm just going to get out with her," I said as I eased Erin slowly out of the car. I got out with her on the passenger side. All three of them then encircled us there.

"Get down on your knees," the bald one firmly instructed us.

Erin and I both collapsed, like altar boys saying their prayers. I was shaking. I reached for her hand, but the Latino slapped mine with his gun, indicating to keep my hands above my head. Erin kept looking forward into the headlights. Purposely blinding herself from our impending executions. I did the same.

A car door opened and shut. Out of the headlights a fourth guy slowly approached. Taking his time. Clearly the leader of the group. He was better dressed as well. Cowboy boots, dress pants, and a tan corduroy blazer. His skin was light, but he appeared to be Latino also, with dark eyes and dark slicked-back hair. Middle-aged. He stepped between the three and stood right in front of us.

"Are you Alex?" he asked me, with a south-of-the-border accent. We were looking right at each other.

"I am. I'm the one you're looking for. My girlfriend has nothing to do with this."

"I know that," he replied, and he looked over at Erin and then turned back toward me. "Both of you stand up." We did as he said and slowly lowered our arms down to our sides. The lieutenants patted us down to check for weapons. "I need answers from you, Alex. I need the truth, okay?"

"OK."

"Good. Now we are on the same page." He reached into his pocket and grabbed a pack of cigarettes. He lit one. "Our friend Carter has been stealing from me for some time now. He blamed it on you, Alex, and the one before you." His broken English was fully audible.

"I never stole anything. It's not true," I said, emphatically denying Carter's claim.

"Shh, shh, shh. I not even finish. It's okay, Alex. I know Carter was lying to me. His whole story of needing mules like you never added up. He used you and your predecessor. A scapegoat I think how you say."

"I'm not sure what you mean," I said, and then as soon as those words came out of my mouth I regretted it. They could be taken as a sign of disrespect. But he smiled and looked at his lieutenants, and they also eased up a little. Another toke on his cigarette. Smoke going upward and disappearing like water poured on sand.

"Alex, I been in this business a long time. When it doesn't add up, then something's wrong. Someone cut my coke. I always get pure coke, Alex. But someone put cut into it. Cheated me out of my money. When I asked Carter, he blamed his mule. I told him to get a new mule. Next delivery, which was your first, we missing two pounds." I tried to speak, but he raised his hand to signal me to just listen. "We ask him again, and he denied involvement. He blamed you."

He finished his cigarette and looked at his watch. Reaching back into the inside pocket of his jacket, he pulled out the pack of cigarettes. "One for the lady," he said to Erin. Surprisingly she accepted, and he lit it for her. "Fool me once, shame on me. Fool me twice, shame on you. That's my favorite American saying. See, we learned that our friend Mr. Pate make some bad business decisions, Alex, and he owe the wrong kind of people a lot of money." He turned from us and walked back to his silver Mercedes. He opened the back door, reaching in. He came back to us carrying a suede jacket, draping it over Erin's shoulders. "How's that?" he asked.

"Thank you," Erin replied.

"Do you have my coke, Alex?" he asked. It caught me by surprise. His tone became more serious. All business.

"I don't have it on me, but I can get it for you." I kept it short. Not knowing what he knew or what he'd believe.

He looked at his watch, and then he looked at the bald-headed man. The silence was tough to handle. Erin looked at me. Wanting me to explain things. Say more. But for some reason, maybe instinct, I thought that I had said enough.

"Okay, Alex, you go get the coke and meet me at Ruedi Dam tomorrow night at eight. Do you know this place?" he asked.

"I'm familiar with it, but it will take me two days to get the coke. It's up in the mountains, and I have to hike in to get it." I knew I was pushing him with my reply, but it was the truth, and I was hoping that he could see it in my eyes. See it in my clothes and face and hands. The dirt. The grit. Telling him the story, as unbelievable as it would've sounded to him, was my next option.

He began speaking Spanish with his lieutenants. All three of them engaging in a conversation. Their thoughts hidden in a foreign language. Increasing my anxiety. Erin moved closer to me. The skin of her arm sticking out from under the suede jacket and touching mine. She felt cold. It felt like it was all just a bad dream. The lights in our eyes. Words from strangers from another world that we could never imagine meeting. Paths crossing on a late-night mountain road. I kept hoping to wake up. And then he switched back to English and turned his attention toward me. We were the same height. Eye to eye.

"You have an *ángel de la guarda*, my friend," he said and smiled. His lieutenants chuckled. "I give you until eight o'clock the following night." He looked at his watch again. "That about forty hours. Okay, Alex?"

It was the best deal I was going to get. No matter what I told him. The whole story or just part of it. Or even something make-believe. What had happened in my world, or even the outside world, would be of little interest to them. This was business. Two million dollars' worth. They wanted every penny. And they wanted their pride intact. To them, they were one and the same.

I asked no questions about Carter. As he had said, Carter had borrowed money from the wrong people, and for all I knew that had run its course. Perhaps coincidence that they were now here at the same time. Maybe he had told me part of the story so that I could understand Carter's motive for stealing from them. That they were not in the wrong on this. That they had not started this. A sort of attempt to let me know that things could be resolved from here if we all were honest with one another and we all ended up with what we wanted. That was what I wanted to believe. But no matter what I wanted to believe, the reality was that we were being held against our will at gunpoint by people who were seedier than they portrayed themselves to be. They were not honest businesspeople. No criminal could be. He was a good salesman. The cigarettes. The jacket for Erin. The calm voice amid the chaos of being abducted from our car. Seemingly a voice of reason. But it all changed when two of them suddenly grabbed Erin and the bald man stuck his pistol onto my forehead.

"What the fuck are you doing?" were the only words I could get out before the blow to my stomach took the wind from me and I dropped to the ground. I could see Erin being put into the car. She let out a scream, but then they covered her mouth and shoved her into the backseat of the Mercedes.

"Listen to me, Alex. I like you, and I no want to harm you or your girl," he said, as the bald man stood right next to him with his gun trained on me. "So again, Alex, you know where Ruedi Dam is, right?" I nodded my head, letting him know that I did. "Okay, Alex. Take the road to the dam, and we be waiting for you." He then quickly spoke Spanish to the bald man. "It's pretty there at sunset. Bring me my coke and you get your girl back. Simple as that. Okay, Alex?"

"Don't hurt her," I said gasping for air.

"I am a man of my word, Alex. A businessman. No harm to her as long as you bring me my coke. I see you soon."

They walked to their car and got in and backed away. I watched them from the pavement. A sickening low. Watching Erin being taken away. Kicking and screaming and terrified. What had I done? It was all because of me.

CHAPTER THIRTY-SEVEN

I got back on my feet and into Erin's Jeep. Making a checklist in my mind, I realized that I had left my backpack in Megan's car. A complete oversight on my part. Preoccupied with my brief reunion with Erin and forgetting my most valuable and important possession. I carefully turned the car around and then drove back up the mountain. Parked in front of the garage. Blocking Erin out of my mind. Thinking of her was debilitating, and I couldn't afford to be that way. Time was of the essence.

Megan heard the car and flipped on the outside lights. She was waiting for me at the front door.

"I left my backpack in your car," I said to her.

"Oh, no problem. Hang on and I'll go around and open the garage door for you."

I waited for it to open. When it did I walked in and grabbed it out of the backseat. Megan stood in the doorway that led into the house. She could see that Erin's car was empty.

"Where's Erin?"

"We got into a little argument, and she's waiting for me at the bottom of your driveway. She wanted to have a cigarette and look at the stars…away from me for a few minutes." Another one of my lies.

"You bes' be nice to her," Megan instructed me as she cracked a little smile. "Tell her to call me in the morning."

"OK, thanks again for everything."

Adrenaline kept me awake on the road. The gas station in Carbondale was open twenty-four hours. It hadn't been that long since I had stopped in. A place I would normally never give much thought to. Even look down upon for keeping its doors open around the clock. There in small-town Colorado. All lit up like a lucky star. Mine. It would have the food and water I needed. And I had enough money left over from Warren to pay for it all. I pulled in.

Somewhere along the way I had to pull over and sleep, though it was the last thing I wanted to do. The clock was ticking. But I knew I needed rest before the long hike ahead. I put the backseat down and curled up in the back of the Cherokee.

It was daylight when I came to. Still early morning, so I wasn't panicked. The few hours of sleep were just what I needed. Then, as big as billboards, came thoughts of Erin. I couldn't believe how overwhelming they were.

I reached the totem pole that signaled the turnoff to Warren Piersma's cabin at eight thirty. I was certain he would be on his way to Telluride, so I didn't hesitate turning into it. When I reached the cabin his Suburban wasn't there. It was vacant. My hopes rested on finding an open door or window, and then finding a hidden firearm inside. I didn't want to go back up into the mountains without a gun.

They might still be up there. The image of them with their weapons on that bank fifty feet away from me. Heart starts beating faster. But the door and windows were locked and the only way in was to break and enter, which I wasn't going to do the property of someone who had given me so much help. Finding a gun was a longshot anyway.

With my backpack loaded up and firmly on my back, I set off to follow the creek upstream. My goal was to reach the rocky outcrop where I had hidden the coke by sunset. There was no room for error. No getting lost this time. The water was my trail. It would be hard going traveling against the current at times. Wading upstream in waist-deep water when the shoreline wasn't available in the canyons. But it was the surest bet of finding my way back.

It was clearly visible there from high up on the bank. Looking like a forehead of granite in a face of evergreens. The outcrop. Swollen. Half sun. Half shade. Seeing it made me feel the same way I did when I first laid eyes on Erin. Full of hope. I smiled and rested. Keeping my eyes on it. Enjoying the view and mapping my route up to it. A few hours at most. Right on schedule.

I beat the setting sun. Making it to the outcrop and over its ridge with the last bit of daylight draining away like the sweat on my body. I felt incredibly high. The outline of where Sarah and I had slept was still there in the dirt. I made my way to the back side of the outcrop and located the ledge with the little pine growing out of it. The rocks were still up there too. It looked untouched. Relief. I took off my backpack and climbed up. Moved the rocks over and carefully removed the dirt with my hand spade and hands. It was there, just as I had left it. All wrapped up in plastic. I scooped it out and climbed back down. Securing it in the middle pouch of my backpack. Triumph. I had done it. There was so much energy and excitement surging through me. Bordering on pride, if such a thing could be felt considering the circumstances.

There was no way I was bedding down anywhere nearby for the night. The memories of the area still haunted me. And I was in no mood to try and sleep. It was almost as if I had the coke running through my body. I was wired. Ready to make the trek back. At least as far as the river. But I only had a half hour of sunlight. That would determine where I ended up, whether or not I had the energy to continue on.

I stretched the visibility as best I could. Going well beyond an hour. It became too dark to make my way without a flashlight, and using one was not an option. Ever present was a healthy fear of who may be around me. Along with the implications of getting lost. There was no reason to go farther other than my own impatience. After filling up on peanut-butter-and-cheese crackers, exhaustion set in and I lay down. I remember looking up at all the millions of stars and thinking about Erin. And then at some point just shutting my eyes.

I dreamed of Sarah. In the dream she was calling out my name. Over and over from higher up in the mountains. An image of her curled up in red snow and shivering in the same spot where she died. Over and over she kept calling my name and asking me to help her.

There was sweat on my forehead when I awoke. I could feel a drop of it sliding down the side of my face. The stars were still shining. I shut my eyes, and Sarah called my name again. It seemed so real. Her voice, and the image of her balled up was as if I was still right there with her. I opened my eyes to make it stop.

I stayed awake for the rest of the night, and at the first hint of daybreak I was packed up and out of there. On my way home. Back to the creek. Spooking a juvenile black bear on the other side. Watching him scramble up the bank and disappearing into the trees. I traveled as fast as he did. Along that waterway. Only stopping for water and food when absolutely necessary.

The cabin came into view, and I looked at my watch. It was 3:00 p.m. Ahead of schedule. I saw Erin's Jeep, and it's hard to describe the feeling I had. Something of hers. A feeling of both home and freedom. When I reached the car I kicked off my wet boots and socks and threw them into the back. I changed shirts, putting on the less rancid of the two, and then tossed the backpack into the back. The side mirror gave me a glance of myself. A raw appearance. A face of dirt and hair.

By the side of the cabin, I saw a blue plastic tarp that was bunched up on the ground with some rocks and dirt on it. Something old and discarded by Warren. It had use for me. I cleaned it up and then brought it over to the Jeep. I took the coke out of my backpack and wrapped it all up in the tarp. Nice and tight. It now had multiple layers of plastic on and around it. It fit on the floor of the backseat and was out of view with the backseat folded down over it. The only things visible in the back were my backpack, socks, and boots. Thinking of any ways I could err on the side of caution while being on the road with the cargo that had to make it to Ruedi Dam by eight o'clock.

The traffic was medium, and I was happy to never pass even one police, sheriff, or state trooper. The biggest problems were slow-moving cars and trucks. They seemed to be constant. As much as I wanted to pass them,

I remained patient and avoided anything that I could get pulled over for. Anything that could possibly cause a wreck. Slow and steady. The speed limit or even below. I had time to spare, even though I felt like a horse spotting the barn at the end of a long ride. The AM radio helped with the pace.

The gas station at Carbondale was like the white flag at Indy. The final lap. I reached it at six o'clock. Only two hours away from Erin and putting everything behind us. I pulled in and pumped four dollars' worth of gas into the tank. That was all the money I had left over from the twenty that Warren had given me. I wanted to wash my hands and clean up a little in the station restroom, but I wasn't going to let the car and what was in it out of my sight.

It was a short ride up to Basalt. The junction of the Frying Pan and Roaring Fork Rivers. I turned onto Frying Pan Road and began my ascent up to the Ruedi Reservoir Dam. It was a truly beautiful stretch of road. Hugging the Frying Pan River with each twist and turn. I had been up and down it many times. Knew the area well from all the summers spent out there with my family. Always in search of the giant trout that had an endless supply of food pumping out from the dam. A buffet line. All they had to do was hold stationary in the current and slurp in the aquatic insects that bounced along the bottom of the river. Haphazardly tossed from the stillness of the bottom of the reservoir and into the vacuum of the fast-moving stream. Tumbling and tumbling in hopes of lodging onto a submersed stone, gravel, or boulder. Any place but the open mouth of a trout.

A couple miles up the road I pulled into a turnout that fishermen often used when vacant. There was a nice pool below that always held a few trout. It was a place where I could rinse off without losing sight of the car. I pulled the keys out of the ignition and didn't bother to put them in my pocket. Anything could happen with them on me. They could fall out of my pockets. Fall into the river. It was safer to leave them under a rock right next to the Jeep. I wasn't taking any chances.

The cold water numbed my hands within seconds, but it felt so good. Clean and fresh. I rubbed it all the way up my forearms as I squatted on the bank and rinsed off the dirt. Still in my bare feet. They were next. The smell had become very strong. The water would rinse some of it away. I was tempted to take all of my clothes off and get into the stream to wash off, but there was a risk of the fish and game warden seeing me or anyone seeing me and being offended. I wasn't going to do anything that would call attention to myself.

I climbed up the bank using the smoothest stones. They were more comfortable on my feet. Back on the road I went farther up toward the dam. Every so often passing a fisherman in the water or in his truck or car. The red rocks on the hills losing their color, and the pines taking over and turning the surrounding mountains green. The result of the gain in elevation.

The small parking area by the Ruedi Dam sign was empty. Sometimes I had seen it with a car or two. Tourists stopping for a photo of the lake. But it was empty when I reached it and pulled in. It was seven o'clock. I was certain this was the spot where I was supposed to meet. There was another much larger pullout a little bit farther up that stretched along the lake, but I could keep it in sight. Staying put covered all the bases.

Though the area was somewhat remote, it wasn't desolate, and you could count on a car passing by every once in a while. There were no trees or darkly lit areas. It was a wide-open place. A good thing, I thought. A place where an exchange could occur easily, quickly, and quietly. It made sense that he had picked it.

Leaning against the front of the car, I waited. Looking out at the lake and turning around whenever I heard an approaching car. I was just like any other tourist. Enjoying the view. Except I had a million thoughts running around my head. Anxiously waiting to see Erin. To have her back. I had had plenty of time to run through all the contingencies. The worst one being that they never showed up. Erin never came back. But that was so unrealistic. They wanted their coke. That's what it all boiled down to. And there were no police involved. I was sure they were aware that I hadn't run in that direction. They knew I wouldn't do anything that would jeopardize Erin. So I convinced myself that there was nothing to worry about. I was on time. The coke was in the Jeep. They would arrive soon.

They did. To my surprise the silver Mercedes approached from the opposite direction from which I came. I was expecting them to come from Basalt. It pulled into the large turnout that was just up the road and signaled me with a flash of its headlights. It then turned around facing away from me. The car's tinted side and rear windows prevented me from seeing who was inside. I could see that the bald man was driving though. I clearly recognized him. I didn't know what they wanted me to do. Then an arm came out of the front passenger window and signaled me to come to them.

I got in Erin's car and backed out and onto the road. Headed up toward them. As I approached the turnout to pull in behind them, they began to drive. It was clear they wanted me to follow. But where to? I wanted to pull up beside them and demand to see Erin. But I had to be calm. There wasn't much room on that two-lane mountain road anyway. It was not a good idea with the possibility of oncoming traffic at any moment coming around a bend. The car sped up to about thirty-five miles per hour, and I stayed right behind it. Close enough to read its Colorado plates. I didn't like what was happening. We were going farther and farther away from people. People who could help Erin and me if we needed them to.

Frying Pan Road followed the lake. I had only ever been as far as the dam on it. We now had traveled to the other side of the lake. It was far more remote over there. I stayed about thirty yards behind them. Wondering when they would stop or turn onto any of the side roads or drives that we came upon. Farther and farther we went, eventually reaching the opposite end of the lake from the dam. The car's right turn signal came on well in advance of a road I could see up ahead. They turned onto it, and I followed. After a half mile the pavement turned into dirt. Dry dirt. Dust kicked up, and I had to wind up the window. I could feel myself beginning to sweat, and it wasn't from the heat. It was my mind and body in overdrive, along with a sinking feeling that I was driving to my death. That Erin wasn't even alive. My stomach knotted, and my breathing became short and rapid. The closed windows only sealed everything in and worsened my condition. My up-and-down emotions mirroring the mountain road.

The red of their taillights illuminated through the dust and I put my foot on the brake to slow down. We both came to a full stop in a small, empty field. I kept the Jeep running. Sitting behind the wheel. As the dust began to settle down I saw the front doors open, and two of the guys from the night before emerged. The bald man and the younger man with the ponytail. Neither had a weapon that I could see. Both were in jeans and black T-shirts tucked into their pants and wrapped up with a belt. Almost like uniforms except for the difference in color on the jeans and the necklines of the shirts. Black street shoes for the ponytail and the same combat boots still on the bald man with his black goatee.

I turned off the car and got out. At the same time their boss came out of the back of the car with the short Latino guy, and Erin. I began to head toward her, but the bald man and his colleague with the ponytail cut into my path. Clearly I wasn't to go any farther. I played by their rules and stopped.

The businessman stepped out in front and came walking up to me. He had on the same corduroy blazer and cowboy boots. The only thing different was his jeans and his embroidered button-down shirt. He extended his hand for me to shake, which I did.

"Good evening, Alex," he said. "Is this not a beautiful place?" He gestured with his outstretched arms to the mountains surrounding us. His two lieutenants standing right behind him and Erin and the Latino in the rear. I leaned to the left to keep her in my sight.

"I have your coke," I replied, wanting to let him know right away that I had kept my part of the deal. Hoping to have Erin in the Jeep with me and on the road home as quickly as possible.

"That is good news, Alex. How you say, music to my ears." He turned and smiled to his group.

Revealing the location of the coke was like laying my cards down on the poker table. I would have no leverage beyond that point and would be completely at their mercy. I hoped he would honor his deal and be the "honest businessman" he portrayed himself to be. I waited for a moment to see if he would say something or initiate the next move, but since I had spoken first he was smart enough to let me continue moving things forward. He just looked at me and smiled. I relented.

"It's in the car. Bring Erin to me, and then I'll get it." Went with my gut. Firm and fair. You scratch my back, I'll scratch yours.

He turned to his men and began speaking Spanish. When he finished, they halfheartedly laughed. Facing me once again with a smile on his face, he folded his arms across his chest and resumed in English.

"I like you, Alex. I tell my people you belong in our organization," he said, lauding my attempt to stand my ground and asking to receive before giving. "I tell you what, you tell me where it is in your car and one of my people will get it."

"But you said—"

"*Uno momento, mi amigo.* Let me finish. You tell me where it is and then you come over here and be with Erin. Reunite."

"It's under the backseat that's folded down."

He quickly spoke a few words in Spanish. The two guys behind him walked over to the Jeep, and I hurried to Erin's side. Right before I got to her, the Latino let go of her arm and she rushed into me. I held her with all my strength, lifting her off the ground. I heard the Jeep doors open up and then a moment later shut. More Spanish being spoken. The merchandise inspected. If a bullet was going to come, at least I was with Erin and she was with me.

"Alex, I wish you all the best," he said, and then he and the others walked over to the Mercedes. The four of them got into their car and drove away. Erin and I stayed where we were.

"I love you so much. I'm so sorry." She stayed in my arms. Protected from the world. "Are you OK?"

"I'm fine," she whispered into my ear.

"They didn't hurt you, did they?" I wiped her cheeks clean.

"No, they didn't."

The night they took her, she was blindfolded and driven to an isolated house about an hour away from Megan's. That was her best guesstimate of the time spent traveling. They locked her in one of the second floor bedrooms, and kept her there. She assured me she was OK and wasn't mistreated. But it was obvious that she had been emotionally drained over those forty-eight hours, knowing that everything was dependent on my return. She did her best to hide the suffering she endured, but I knew it went deep, and all I could do was hold her in my arms and share it with her until the tears stopped. When they did we walked over and got into the front seats of her Jeep. I put my arms around her, but I didn't feel her doing the same.

"What's wrong?" I asked her as I unwrapped my arms and sat back behind the wheel. She kept her head down. Not looking at me. "Erin," I said to her in an attempt to get her to look at me with her pretty blue eyes.

"I keep thinking about Sarah Evans and her family. And Carter."

I looked out the windshield. I knew where she was coming from because I felt the same. But not about Carter, and I was surprised she brought up his name.

"You heard what the drug boss said about Carter," I said. "He was using me. I believe what he told us. It makes sense." I reached over and touched her face. Began putting my arm around her. Drawing her nearer. I could feel though she still wasn't willing to give in. "And we don't know what happened to him. For all we know he owed the wrong type of guys a lot of money, and maybe they were the ones who killed him."

"So you're putting faith in the words of some drug dealer from another part of the world," Erin replied. "Someone who kidnapped me. Held me hostage. I was so frightened, Alex. You have no idea what I went through, not knowing what was going to happen, and you think everything is fine because we're back together and physically unharmed."

She was right. I had forgotten about the past and began thinking about our future. We would just move on. Whatever scars were on my back would heal and only be seen by those behind me. But it was obvious things were not the same for Erin. I got out, went to the back of the car, and reached into one of the pockets of the backpack where there was a picture of us that I had put inside two Ziploc baggies. Luckily it had stayed dry. I pulled it out and then returned to the front seat.

"Remember this from our ski trip to Stratton Mountain?" I handed the picture to her. She took it out of my hand. Looked at it. Dried her tears. A smile began appearing on her face. "Whenever I go anywhere and I know I'm not going to see you for a while, I take this with me. It's my favorite picture of us. Nothing will ever change the way I feel when I look at it."

She leaned a little closer, and then I put my arm around her again. There was more of a feeling of warmth from her. But until she was willing to put her arms around me as well, I knew that she was still battling her emotions. Conscience. I had said what I needed to say, and I thought it was simply a matter of time. Of her dealing with this at her own pace.

"We have to do something for Sarah and her husband. It's just going to continue to eat at me if we don't," she said, softly tucked under my arms.

"I know we do," I told her truthfully.

"We have to do something now, Alex."

"OK, we will." I continued to keep her wrapped up in my arms in the fading light.

We locked the doors and climbed into the back of the Jeep, both of us too physically and mentally exhausted to drive home, or anywhere. I rolled out the sleeping bag. The two of us got in. Curled up. In that position it was impossible not to think of Sarah. Maybe Erin was thinking the same since I had told her everything I went through. Neither of us mentioned her name. Her presence went unspoken. But she was definitely there. Somewhere between us. And as the night worked as silently as anesthesia to erase the world around us, and then leave us there side by side, what little energy we had left from our ordeal dissipated and we soon drifted off to sleep.

Several hours later, in the middle of the night, I could feel that Erin had awakened, as I had done, and that we were both just lying there. Eyes open in the dark like twins in the womb.

"Are you awake?" I whispered.

"Yes."

"Are you thinking about Sarah too?"

"Yes." So faint.

"There's something I didn't tell you about, and only because it's just a little detail, and because I'm not really sure what it means."

"What is it?"

I turned over onto my back. Unzipping the sleeping bag to allow me to move. My knees having to stay bent and upright because of the limited space. She remained on her side facing away from me.

"There was something that I found that Sarah had carved into a rock, and I think about it from time to time, like I'm doing now. It was the last thing she said to me."

She rolled over onto her back, paused for a moment, and then turned onto her side facing me. Her arm draped over my chest and rested there.

"What did it say?"

"It was just her name spelled out and then some numbers and letters," I told her, and then I spelled it out for her as it was written, SEVANS GLS308. "She was obviously wanting to let anyone who might ever come across it know that she had been there."

"Why would she leave out her first name?" Erin asked. "How would anyone know who SEvans was?"

"I don't know," I said, as my wheels continued to turn. "Maybe she didn't have time. Only enough time for the abbreviation. I remember her telling me how she thought they were going to kill her after she was caught trying to escape."

Erin thought for a minute. "Then that would mean the last part was more important to her than her first name. What were the numbers and letters again?"

I told them to her. I knew them backward and forward because they stuck with me when I came across them and tried to figure out what they meant. "I've been thinking that it has something to do with March 8. I don't know if that's her birthday or something else," I said, and I turned back onto my side facing her. My right arm around her. Keeping her warm. Keeping her forehead nestled against my neck and breathing over the top of her. It had been several days since I had brushed my teeth, and the stubble on my face was rough.

We both ran through anything that could be significant with March 8. But everything that we came up with didn't make the cut. We then moved on from thinking 308 was a date to possibly an address. Her street number in Wyoming. But if she used that as an identifier, then it wasn't that much of a time saver over her first name of Sarah. So we ruled that out as well. The GLS maybe stood for three words beginning with each of those letters. Or maybe initials of someone's name. We kept at it. Each coming up with reasonable possibilities but none that jumped out at us. Then Erin sat up. Climbed out of the sleeping bag. Folded her arms around her knees, which she had raised up.

"What if it's a license plate number?" she said.

Then I realized what Erin was thinking. Sarah wasn't going to just accept her fate. She was going to do everything she could to win back her freedom, and at the least, she was going to make sure that those responsible for taking it away would be held accountable. It was the license plate of her abductors. That's what she was trying to tell me. That's what her last words about the rock meant. I was sure of it. I grabbed the flashlight and got out of the car, Erin right behind me. I shone it on our rear Colorado plate. The new one Erin had recently put on the Cherokee to become a more official resident of the state. The sequence of our own letters and numbers convinced us even more.

We got back into the Cherokee and climbed into the sleeping bag. Seeking warmth. The cool mountain air nearing its lowest temperature in the predawn hours and forcing us to take shelter. I had contemplated starting the car and turning on the heat for Erin, but I liked the solitude we had found, and an engine could attract attention. We were either on private or public land, neither of which—I was certain—allowed vehicles to remain overnight without a permit. It was best to remain unnoticed. Body heat would do. The down bag was sufficient. It would just take a little time.

"How are we going to let the police know?" she asked me.

It was a good question, and I was hoping there was a way to come forward while also remaining in the shadows. "The problem with me showing up at the police station is that I lied to the State Trooper when he pulled me over on 82. What if for some reason they're able to connect the dots back to Carter? Then I'm fucked."

Erin sort of nodded in agreement. "But what other way is there?"

My wheels were turning. "What if I send the cops an anonymous letter? I could go to the library in town and type something up letting them know what I saw and where Sarah's body is. As best as I could tell them. Maybe even draw a map. I could drop it into a mailbox down in Glenwood or even farther away to make sure they would never know who sent it. Scotch tape my fingertips too."

"And you'd include the license plate number, right?" she said, making sure I didn't leave out such an important part.

"Yes, of course," I assured her. She turned back toward me. I pulled her in close.

When sunrise came, we started up the Jeep and began our drive back to Aspen. We drove around Ruedi Reservoir and then followed the Frying Pan down to Basalt. The fly fishermen in their favorite holes and runs. Fly lines rolling out on the forward and back casts. Tight loops the shape of paper clips. The thin monofilament ready to drop a fly the size of a pupil onto the surface of the water. Man versus trout. I watched each one as they came into view on our way down to 82.

"I need to call work. They're going to be wondering where I am." Erin said out of the blue. I needed to do the same. I had completely forgotten about our jobs. The rest of the world.

I saw a line come tight. The rod quickly placed high in the air. The tip of it bending.

CHAPTER THIRTY-EIGHT

The reunion with our apartment was a true homecoming. Our own place. The smell of the flowers that Erin always kept by the kitchen window. Her impressionist painting of Bow Bridge in Central Park hanging over the fireplace. The books. Colors. Her slippers on the floor in the living room. For a moment I indulged, whether I had earned it or not.

Drawing the razor blade across my face was such a luxury. Dipping it continuously into the warm water in the sink. Smooth skin unearthed with each stroke. Standing there in my boxers. A hot shower came next. Soap. Lots of it. The stubborn dirt beneath my nails. Little slices of the bar getting stuck below each one and then melting away.

Dripping down my fingers. Repeating the process until no black remained. Clean as could be.

The steam rose to the ceiling and fanned out from there. The exhaust vent had never worked, so the steam would eventually build up and form a cloud. Always reminding me of the first time I looked out a jet window on a trip with my dad when I was eight years old. He had taken me to New York City on business. With my face in the water, I daydreamed about it. Visiting his customers with him in my little business suit. A replica of my dad. One-fifth the size. The sights and sounds of the city. Taxis blowing horns. People everywhere. Talking. He held my hand. Never letting go. The giant hotdog he bought me right by the carousel in Central Park. It was the best thing I had ever eaten.

The hot water began running out, so I turned the cold completely off. I would stay in the shower as long as it remained warm. To the last drop. It felt so amazing. My mind drifting off to New York City and then other childhood memories. Peaceful. Warm.

When the hot ran out, I turned off the water and grabbed a towel. Another luxury. Soft cotton. Erin always loved big, soft towels, and she would wrap herself up in one after her shower or bath.

In the steam-filled room I took the towel to wipe off a portion of the mirror above the sink so that I could see myself, still dripping water all over the tiled floor. Magically my face appeared. The bathroom was warm, but I knew it would not stay that way once I opened the door. It would all clear. Cooler air rushing in from the bedroom. The open window letting in the Aspen morning air.

I put the towel around me and went into the bedroom. Erin had gotten a fire going in the fireplace. I could smell it in our room. The towel was replaced with fresh boxers, shorts, and a T-shirt, and then I went back into the bathroom to brush my teeth. Loading up on the toothpaste. It had been days. When I finished and the mint flavoring lingered so strongly I could almost feel it, I grabbed a comb and quickly brushed my hair and parted it on the side. Completing the image that I approved of in the mirror.

She was sitting on the floor right by the fireplace. She had changed clothes. Into her favorite black cotton sweater and a fresh pair of jeans. Bare feet. Her old self, but attire only. She just kept looking at me.

"What?" I asked her, standing there at the edge of the living room. Not moving.

No reply. Kept looking at me with sadness on her face. I sat down on the couch. The fire had taken hold. Logs burning. The purple of the flame so hypnotizing. "I'm just so overwhelmed by everything. It's hitting me all at once right now, I guess."

"Erin, look at me. I'm so sorry. It crushes me to see you this way, and I know it's all my fault."

She turned away and looked at the fire. "I just can't believe you lied to me. And for so long."

"I don't know what to say."

"You don't have to say anything. Let's just do what we can to help Sarah and her husband, and their families. I feel so sorry for them."

"I do too. I'll take care of it now."

I stood up. Went into the bedroom and got my wallet and Rossignol baseball cap. My car keys were on the kitchen counter, and I grabbed my jean jacket from the hall closet. Erin met me at the door and hugged me.

I leaned down and gave her a kiss goodbye. "See you soon," she said.

I knew where the police station was, but I didn't have the address, so that was my first stop. While driving by it I wrote down the numbers and street. Kept moving. Out of town. I pulled into the first gas station I saw. Ten bucks' worth of gas. Cleaned the windshield while it pumped. Back onto Highway 82 and headed for Glenwood. Their library would be open by the time I got down there. Aspen's was still closed.

It was a beautiful morning. Bright sunshine. Mid-fifties. I drew up the letter in my head as I drove with the mountain air rushing in on me. It wouldn't need to be long. Though I knew that the people who read it would have many questions. I would do my best to answer them. I could get it all in on a single page. Typed on a publicly used machine. I could do it unnoticed right when the library opened. Uncrowded. I could pick up the envelope at K-Mart in Glenwood. I could also purchase the stamp at the post office in town. And I decided I would make the drive over to Dillon and mail it there. Putting even more distance from my identity. The town was right off I-70. Thousands of people drove by it every day going east and west through the Rockies. I was one in a million. It was a solid plan. Maybe even a little too cautious, but I was willing to literally go the extra mile to remain anonymous.

After my quick stops at K-Mart and the post office, I pulled into the library. It was as deserted as I had expected it to be. It had two typewriters side by side in the rear of the building. Sitting on their own little tables. In the back of the section where the magazines and newspapers were kept. Hidden in a way. Neither was in use. Nearby was the copy machine, and underneath the cabinet it sat on was a package of copy paper. I grabbed a sheet.

What I had written in my head did not transfer easily onto the paper. Like my mind was playing a game of charades with my fingers. The page remained empty except for the introduction of a hiker on a journey through the Roaring Fork Watershed. It had been so much easier to write while driving down Highway 82. The more I thought about things, and second-guessed myself, the tougher it became to draft the letter. There was also the pressure of the clock. I had wanted to get in and out of the library quickly. Avoiding people. And just the opposite was occurring as I sat stuck in neutral with the library gradually becoming more and more active. But a few moments later I calmed down and cleared my mind.

It all came out. It wasn't perfectly written, and I know I left some things out, but most all of it was there. I was certain the details would allow them to draw a clear picture of what had happened to Sarah, and hopefully who it was that took her. Certainly they would run the license plate number in multiple states. Or every state. And a name would jump at them. The break they were looking for. And I did my best to direct them to Sarah's body. Her remains. The river. The rocky outcrop that was a giant bulge of granite that so prominently stood over the valley. The landmark they could use to find her, even though I didn't come upon her corpse on my return trip.

At the end of the letter I expressed my wish to remain anonymous for fear of retribution from the accused. It was a legitimate reason for not wanting to get involved. Believable. They would just have to accept it because the author was not coming forward and revealing himself, cowardly as that may seem.

I typed up the address of the Aspen Police Department on the envelope and then left the library thirty minutes after my arrival there. Back in my car and heading eastward. Through Glenwood Canyon. Over the Vail Pass. The descent down to Dillon where the Blue River flows.

It was an almost three-hour drive back to Aspen. Erin was waiting for me with a big brunch she had made. It had started as a breakfast but turned into an assortment of many small things that she cooked while waiting for me to show up. We sat at the dining room table, and I told her about my day. The letter. Passing food back and forth to each other. It almost seemed normal again.

CHAPTER THIRTY-NINE

Three days later Aspen became the epicenter of the search for Sarah Evans. The town swelled with the ranks of various law enforcement personnel and mountain rescue teams. Everyone knew something big was up, but nothing leaked out. People speculated on many things, including rumored narcotics trafficking involving the murder of Carter Pate, which put Alex on edge. But the absence of DEA agents dispelled that. It was something bigger. Alex and Erin knew it had to be about Sarah. The letter had worked.

It didn't take them long to find her. With helicopters and dogs, and Alex's best recollection of where her remains could be found, the odds were in their favor. He was at work when the story broke. It spread like wildfire.

Media personnel from all around streamed into Aspen like a D-Day invasion.

The announcement was made that a special news conference would be held at two o'clock on that Saturday afternoon. Alex called Erin from work. She had already heard the news.

Police Chief Martin Sullivan of the Aspen PD began the news conference on the steps of the police station amid a swarm of media and townspeople.

"It is with great sadness that I can confirm that the body of Sarah Evans of Laramie, Wyoming, has been found. At approximately ten forty-five in the morning, agents from the Federal Bureau of Investigation, along with rangers of the US Forest Service, officers of the Pitkin County Sheriff's Department, and members of Mountain Rescue-Aspen discovered the body in a remote section of the White River National Forest. This case is being treated as an apparent homicide. Right now there are no suspects that we have identified, and federal law enforcement, as well as the Laramie Police Department and Colorado State Patrol, will be conducting a joint investigation and will be briefing members of the media separately. Thank you for your time."

He was immediately bombarded with questions, none of which he answered. He simply tilted his police hat and then turned and walked back into the building. Throngs of reporters rushed him, but they were cut short by the police on hand who then closed the building to the public.

It was the biggest story to hit Aspen in a long while, and everyone started with their theories. Erin and Alex though were the only ones who knew the truth, and even they didn't know all of it.

——✦ ✦——

Information was withheld from the general public because the various law enforcement agencies involved didn't want their suspects to look over their shoulders more than they already were, and go underground. They would be easier to find if they had less to fear. Things were happening behind the public eye that had put the investigation into high gear, and anything that got leaked out would only jeopardize its success. They had run the license plate in several states, and it was from the Colorado report that a match was made. It gave them the name of Lowell Henderson. A man with a record. His whereabouts unknown. The plate was registered to a '79 Dodge pickup, though they were well aware the plate could be on any type of vehicle. A good start though. Excitement built.

When Lamar and Kerrigan got a positive identification on Lowell's photo from Ellie Dempsey, they were certain they had one half of Bonnie and Clyde. Now it was just a matter of finding him—and her—which would be no easy task given the size of the Western United States where they seemed most comfortable and would most likely be. The hunt intensified.

CHAPTER FORTY

She pulled into the downtrodden Saturn Motel just outside of Kingman, Arizona. A motel that had seen better days when Route 66 was in its prime. Like the route, it had fallen into a gradual decline with the construction of the interstates throughout the United States and the so-called bigger, better, faster things that came with them, such as restaurant and hotel chains. So the motel had morphed into a "truckers welcome" kind of place. A one-story, thirty-two-room compound comprised of one L-shaped building with the manager's office attached, and a smaller one that was just straight. The smaller building was halfway coated with fresh paint. Tan on the upper half and robin's-egg blue on the bottom to somewhat resemble its namesake planet. All in preparation for the upcoming Labor Day weekend.

It had been eighteen years since Ruth and Eugene Seyfert put a fresh coat of paint on their motor lodge, and when the Mexican painting crew offered them a price that was a third of what every other bid had come in at, they opted to make the investment in their business they had owned for thirty-seven years. Ruth Seyfert even offered to allow the six-man crew free room and board and a home-cooked meal each night for the weeklong project. It would help clear her guilty conscience for the paltry labor rate she was paying.

It was a gray, two-door 1981 Chevy Impala: a nondescript car that blended right in. The parking space in front of the office was open, and the vehicle pulled into it. Ruth took her bowl of leftover chili that she had made for the painters and put it down below the counter. Out of sight. A swipe of the napkin across her lips to clean any food from her face. At seventy-two, she still maintained an unblemished first impression.

Through the picture-frame window, she watched a woman half her age look into the rearview mirror and apply lipstick before opening the car door and heading for the office. Her carefree stroll reminded Ruth of her own gait back in the day. Purse in tow. Black hair, so perfectly black it almost didn't look real. Slender legs in jean cutoffs and cowboy boots that showed a hint of muscle with each stride.

It was dusk in the outskirts of Kingman when she came through the door to check into the Saturn Motel. The neon rings around the "o" in Motel on the twenty-foot sign by the road were just starting to glow brightly against the fast-approaching evening sky.

"Welcome to the Saturn," Ruth said with her customary smile and perfect posture.

"Hi, ma'am, do you have a room available?" the woman asked, though it was obvious by the lack of cars around the motor lodge and the few trucks that were parked over in the truck parking area that it was more a question of how many rooms were available.

"We sure do. How many nights will you be staying?"

"Oh, probably just one night."

"Alright, how many are in your party?" Ruth asked. Even though she saw her pull in by herself, she always went through her standard list of questions. It was just good business.

"Just me," replied the happy looking woman. The woman who took Ruth back forty years.

"I have room eighteen available. It has a king bed and is seventeen dollars plus tax. It's just down a little ways, and you won't be near the painters in the morning. We're putting a new coat of paint on the motel," she said with a hint of pride. "That work for you?"

"How far down is it?"

Ruth pulled out the map of the motel and placed it on the counter, turning it around so that the woman had the correct view of it.

"We're here in the office," she said, pointing with her finger, "and eighteen is down here just before the bend. Right in the middle of the motel."

"That'll be just fine."

"Will you be paying with cash or credit card?"

"Cash."

She signed into the motel after paying Ruth and then was given the key to her room. Ruth noted the name Andrea Bennett written in ink.

"Welcome to the Saturn, Ms. Bennett. I hope you enjoy your stay."

"Thank you. I'm sure I will." She was about to turn and leave, but then hesitated. "Can you tell me where there's a good place to get a bite to eat around here?"

Ruth directed her to a restaurant that specialized in home cooking. It was where she sent everyone, and not just because her son owned the place. It was good food at a fair price. The woman thanked her and then went back out to her car and drove away in the direction of the restaurant.

⊫⊰ ⊱⊨

It was getting near ten o'clock, the time when Ruth would retreat to the rear of the office suite where she and Eugene called home. The late-shift clerk was due to arrive at any moment. Headlights from a car shone through the window as it turned into the property and headed back toward the center motel rooms. It was Ms. Bennett's Impala from room eighteen.

Ruth came around from the counter and walked over to the door where there was a table with a coffee machine and a few cups on it. At that point she had a full view of both buildings. The car pulled up in front of room eighteen. The woman got out and went and opened up the door to the room. Then a man got out on the passenger side and swiftly followed her in.

In her thirty-seven years as the proprietor, she had seen it all before. This was nothing new. A prostitute and her client. And if that wasn't it, just another customer trying to get a room priced for one occupant instead of two. If it was a criminal act, Ruth preferred they use another motel. If it was dishonesty, she felt cheated. It was part of the motel business though and over time she had learned to live with it.

The office phone rang at 10:20 p.m. The night clerk was sick and wouldn't be coming in. The second time that month that he had called in at the last minute to say he wouldn't be coming to work due to an illness. It put her in a tough spot because it was too late to find a replacement for him. It meant that she and her husband would have to split the shift, each of them only getting a few hours of sleep for the night. At their age, that was tough. It was times like these that Ruth gave thought to selling the business. Eventually she knew they would have to. Her only son didn't want any part of it. He was happy with his restaurant, and the few spare hours that he had outside of it were spent raising his three small kids. He had grown up with the motel and had now moved on. It would have to be an outside buyer. Most likely a competitor. Maybe even one of the big chains, who would completely renovate it or raze it and start from scratch. They had the capital to do things like that.

She went back to the living quarters to inform Eugene of the predicament they were in. He offered to take over right away if she needed it. She told him that she would be fine until two o'clock, and then she would come wake him for his shift. He walked into the office and put some coffee on for her while she used the restroom. He didn't move nearly as well as Ruth as he was seven years her senior. She would be the one to take care of him when the time came, which wasn't too far down the road. When she finished she put him to bed, kissing him on the forehead and then turning off the light in the bedroom. There was a mystery novel she was reading, and she picked it up off the small coffee table and brought it with her out into the office. Shutting the door to the living quarters behind her. The quiet helping Eugene to fall asleep. Like a sentry she took her spot on the stool behind the counter with the determination to man her post until it was her time to be relieved of duty. A good book helping her endure the loneliness. The night. Waiting for the next traveler to pull off the highway and become a patron of the Saturn Motel.

After a few pages she looked over at the registration book that contained the name, address, vehicle make and model, and license plate number of each guest. There was something about Andrea Bennett that kept bothering her, and more than just the way she had snuck the man into her room. Sitting there covering the late shift, Ruth had plenty of time to think about it.

She picked up the mystery novel and continued reading. After finishing a short chapter, she turned the opened book upside down and set it on the counter to keep from losing her place. She got up and walked over by the window and door to get a cup of coffee. As she finished pouring she saw the woman come out of eighteen. A bath towel draped over her right hand and almost dragging on the ground. She quickly went to the trunk of the car and opened it. With the towel in her hands she bent over, and for a moment, her upper body disappeared from Ruth's view. When she stood back up, and became fully visible again, there was an object wrapped up in the towel and the woman shut the trunk and hurried back into the room. Ruth stood there for a moment sipping her coffee. Thinking. Watching. To see if anything more was going to transpire out her window. Halfway through her cup she returned to her desk and picked up the phone. The number to the Mohave County Sheriff's Office was on a laminated card along with five other important numbers. The dispatcher answered the call. She knew Ruth and Ruth knew her. Acquaintances.

"Angela, this is Ruth over at the Saturn, and I've got something I'd like you to check out for me."

"Sure, Ruth, what do you have?"

"I've got a guest and my gut tells me something just isn't right with her. Do you have a pen handy?"

"I'm ready," replied the dispatcher.

"Colorado plate GLS308 on an Impala, and she signed the log book as Andrea Bennett, 163 Alpine Lane, Eagle, Colorado. See what you make of this, if you don't mind."

"Will do, Ruth. Give me a little time and I'll be back with you. It's been a busy night with the wreck out on I-40."

"I didn't hear about that. Sure hope nobody's hurt."

"Doesn't appear to be anything too serious, but the traffic is backed up. I would think some of them would be heading your way."

Wrecks and construction were good for business. They prompted people to call it a day or night and get a motel instead of painfully waiting in traffic for who knows how long. Ruth expected to be seeing customers soon, and that would keep her busy. Keep her awake. Add to the bottom line. And as long as nobody was seriously hurt, then she didn't look at it as her benefiting at someone else's expense. She was simply providing a service and had no control of what went on out on I-40.

Twenty minutes had passed when the phone rang and Ruth picked it up.

"Good evening, Saturn Motel, how may I help you?"

"Is this Ruth Seyfert?" a man's deep voice asked, pronouncing her last name as *sea* and *fort*, which was close enough for Ruth.

"Yes, it is, how may I help you?"

"My name is Agent Russ Lamar with the FBI, and I need to ask you a few questions."

His tone was extremely serious. She knew right away it had something to do with the call she had made to the sheriff's office about the woman in room eighteen.

"Please, go right ahead," said Ruth.

"We've been contacted by the Mohave County Sheriff's Office in regard to a license plate number that you phoned in to them a short while ago. I'd like for you to repeat the number to me."

She reached for the piece of paper with the number on it.

"Here it is. Colorado plate GLS308."

The agent used his military background to phonetically repeat what Ruth had told him.

"That's correct," she confirmed.

The FBI had scoured the Western U.S. in their hunt for the killers of five innocent people. Methodically they networked themselves into every law enforcement agency in Wyoming, Montana, Idaho, Nevada, Utah, Colorado, Arizona, New Mexico, California, and Oregon. Lowell Henderson had a history in those areas, and it was likely that he would be there somewhere. Somewhere in the mountains. He and Bonnie. But "somewhere" was their biggest challenge. The search area was more than one million square miles. Endless forests, mountains, deserts, and out-of-the-way places for someone to disappear in. Without a trace. Remain hidden. And in addition to the massive landscape, there were numerous small rural towns and major metropolitan areas in which to take up residence like pennies in a jar. The task was daunting, to say the least. But they were still convinced that it was only a matter of time until Lowell would make a mistake. Their job was to have everything ready when they did, which is what took place when Ruth called the sheriff's office.

With the confirmation of the license plate Ruth gave him, Agent Russ Lamar set the wheels in motion for the apprehension of one of the most wanted criminals in the country. It would involve a quick flight from his office in Phoenix to Kingman. He would arrange for his team of six to be met by Las Vegas agents for more support. He would also make sure they were backed up by the Kingman police and the Mohave sheriff's department. They just had to keep things quiet. Anything that could alert Lowell Henderson could aid in his possible escape and endanger the lives of innocent civilians.

"Ruth, the woman driving the car is staying at your motel, correct?" Agent Lamar asked her.

"Yes. She's in room eighteen. And there's a man with her."

"Can you describe both of them to me?"

"She's about thirty to thirty-five years old. Nice looking. About five foot five with black hair that looks like it's been dyed. I haven't gotten a good look at the fellow with her, but I know he's in the room. Who are they? What have they done?" Ruth asked, wanting to know who these people were that were staying in her motel. It was obvious that this was something serious.

"They are wanted by the FBI. Are they in the motel now?"

"Yes, room eighteen."

"Are there any guests in the rooms next to their room?"

"Not at the moment, but there's a wreck on I-40, and I'm expecting things to pick up soon."

"What are the closest rooms with guests in them?" Agent Lamar asked her. At FBI headquarters, he was directing people to get the plane ready and to get in touch with their Vegas office and the Kingman and Mohave Sheriff's Office. He stood by his desk while talking to Ruth and waving his arm up in the air in a circular motion. They had been working around the clock on this case. Every branch out west had been. They just happened to be the lucky ones receiving the call.

"I've got a couple with their small child in twenty-one and truckers in four, eight, and eleven. Our other building is vacant because it's getting painted in time for the Labor Day weekend. But two of the rooms are being used by the painters."

"How many rooms do you have at your motel?"

"Thirty-two. Twenty-four in our main building and eight in the other."

"How long did they sign in for?"

"You mean Ms. Bennett in eighteen?"

"Yes," the agent replied.

"She paid for just one night."

After getting the information that he needed, Lamar directed Ruth to remain calm and to not do anything that might disturb her visitors in room eighteen; make them nervous and want to leave. Just in case though, he would call the Kingman police and Mohave sheriff to place unmarked vehicles nearby the motel.

"I'll be at your place in about an hour. The Kingman Police Department and the Mohave Sheriff's Department will be in touch with you with further instructions as soon as I hang up. You've done us a tremendous service, ma'am."

CHAPTER FORTY-ONE

Wounds take time to heal, and some leave scars. I tried so hard to put things back together with Erin, but I had broken her trust. Her kiss felt different. Her eyes less revealing. We still lived together, but it never really felt like the two of us were there. It wasn't the same.

When the snow began falling and the ski season arrived, I spent hours on the slopes. I was passionate about the sport. Always trying to improve. Push myself. Praying each night for the opportunity to ski virgin powder in the morning. Make my own tracks. Some days Erin would join me, and afterward we would meet up with our friends at one of the bars. But deep inside our guts underneath our down vests and wool sweaters and nylon ski pants we held a secret that when looking across from each other in a small group of friends always reminded us of what was there. There was no escaping it.

We spent Christmas with our own families. I met my parents and two sisters in New York City. My parents had invited Erin to come, but I told them that she was headed to LA. The separation was painful, like those nights I spent away from her in the wilderness. We talked on the phone but only briefly. Though I wanted to finally get things out on the table with her, I spoke to her mostly in cautious tones. It was Christmas. We were three thousand miles apart, and what needed to be said required eye contact. My stay at the Waldorf ended on the third day when I told my parents that there had been a scheduling mistake at work and that I needed to get back. I could tell though that they knew it wasn't that. They didn't probe. They let me be. They had been young once too.

Aspen was fully booked for the holidays. Like New York City with peaks instead of skyscrapers, it was crowded and congested with money flowing. Our shop was busy, so it was good I had gotten back to help out. All of us worked overtime just to meet the demand. A get-it-while-you-can sort of thing for the local retail businesses. There was no time to ski, but the mountains were so crowded it almost wasn't even worth it anyway.

CHAPTER FORTY-TWO

Agent Lamar and his group of six hustled to the airport and boarded their aircraft for the flight to Kingman. At the same time four agents from Las Vegas were also en route via helicopter. They would meet up at the airport. With the backup of the sheriff's crew and the Kingman police, they would formulate their plan to first identify that the Saturn Motel occupants were who they were looking for, and then capture them. Without loss of life. Their lives or any innocent civilians whom it was their job to protect.

When they landed, the four Vegas agents were waiting for them, the Bell helicopter beating the plane there with less distance to travel. Also at the airport were Mohave

County Sheriff Al Jackson and Kingman Police Chief John Galey. Both the chief and sheriff were in street clothes like the agents. They met in a conference room at the airport under strict security. Not a word was to get out.

Sheriff Jackson had brought a diagram of the motel, which he laid out on the table. There was also a rough sketch of the nearby businesses. Something that the agents could get a quick glimpse of before heading out there.

"My biggest concern is the family in room twenty-one," Lamar told the group as he leaned over the table studying the diagram. He had been unaware of the L shape of the building. Ruth hadn't explained that to him, nor did he think to ask. It presented a problem because it boxed his agents in, and the guests as well, especially those in the nearby rooms like twenty-one. "We need to get them out without alerting our friends in eighteen. I want this done before we even make the positive ID."

"Doing anything with them tonight may get the hair up on their necks," Agent Rory Kerrigan said. He was eager to exact revenge for the families of those killed and wanted nothing more than to be the guy to either collar the criminals or fire the bullets that put them down for good. He lost a brother in high school when a stray bullet from an armed robbery at a convenience store struck him and killed him as he crouched down with others near the front of the store. That incident had prompted Kerrigan to join the FBI when he graduated from college. He had found his calling. Tough and fit and in his late thirties, he had a tempered aggressiveness that served him and the bureau well.

"I hear you but we still need to get them out," said Lamar. "Al and John, let's keep the black-and-whites at least five hundred feet from the motel. Completely out of eyesight from anywhere on the motel grounds. The last thing I want is for this guy to come strolling out of his room in search of the ice machine and see our army parked across the street."

"I've got two of my plainclothes out by the motel now, both on foot, and I know Al has two of his guys in an unmarked cruiser next door at the Marquee in case they run," said Galey, letting the Feds know that he and Jackson hadn't done anything unprofessional. The two of them had many years of law enforcement experience in the Kingman area, and even though they were willing to take a backseat and let the Feds run the show in their own backyard, they wanted to make it known that they were perfectly competent to assist in any way. In their hearts, of course, they actually believed it was a job they could handle themselves and the Feds could've remained in Vegas and Phoenix.

"Great, let's keep them there," Lamar instructed the men. "All right, boys, let's get going."

From the airport, they walked into the waiting cars that Jackson and Galey had arranged for the use of the Feds. The accident out on I-40 forced them to take an alternate route out to the hotel, which would add precious time to their trip. Close to thirty minutes. Anything could happen in that amount of time. Lamar was comforted by the fact that the helicopter was at his disposal if needed, but it was a last resort. He preferred to do things quietly with the element of surprise.

They rode in pairs, following each other. On the way out, Lamar and Kerrigan came up with the idea of possibly using a cleaning lady in the early morning to get an ID on the male occupant. She would have to come from the Kingman police force or the sheriff's department. Preferably fluent in both Spanish and English. An early-morning knock on the door. In broken English or just Spanish expressing the need to deliver fresh towels to the bathroom. A daily requirement of her job. It could work.

It took forty minutes to circumvent the wreck on I-40 using the side roads and city thoroughfares to make it out to the Saturn. The small caravan drove past the motel at normal speeds. Lamar and Kerrigan making all the necessary observations to plan their apprehension. They drove by the unmarked cruiser that was parked as a guest at the Marquee Motel across the street. They also saw one of the undercover officers in his ragged coat, shirt, shorts, sandals, and beard with his booze bottle slouched on the sidewalk a few feet from the parking lot of the Saturn.

A half mile down the road they turned around and then came back and made another pass of the motel. They saw the Impala. Lamar also got his first glimpse of Ruth Seyfert through the office window. The brave woman was doing everything they had instructed her to do. About a mile down the road there was a gap in the businesses. A large abandoned parking lot that was once home to a used car dealership. Lamar pulled into it. The others followed. Everyone got out of the vehicles and walked over to where Lamar was standing with Kerrigan.

"Part of me wants to just wait a few hours until they're asleep and then knock their door down and take them before they even open their eyes. And if it turns out they're not Bonnie and Clyde, then we'll only have to buy the Seyferts a new door," Lamar said to the group. One of the other agents chimed in that he was more than willing to do the same.

But all of them were far too smart to let their emotions interfere with their safety and the safety of the guests in the nearby rooms, and Lamar, being a husband and father of two, was adamant that the family in room twenty-one be moved out before anything was done. He felt the truckers were safe enough where they were.

"Obviously there is too much at risk to do anything before daylight," Lamar said. "As much as I'd like to end this thing sooner, we need to be patient. And we need to get that family out of room twenty-one. Jerry, I'm putting you in charge of that," he said to one of the agents who reported to him in Phoenix. "Al and John, either of you have a female officer who can speak Spanish and English and play the part of a Mexican cleaning lady?"

"I've got a gal who could do that, Russ," said the sheriff.

Lamar and Kerrigan presented their idea for getting a positive ID on the suspects, and after hearing their plan, the sheriff felt sure that he had just the right deputy for the job. After they all conversed more and went over the details, they moved on to the apprehension phase.

"Once we have confirmation on our suspects, we will all move into position and form a secure perimeter. Nobody gets in or out," he said, accentuating his last three words. "We're all on the same page with that, right?" Lamar waited for each one of them to verbally communicate that they understood exactly what he was saying.

They drafted their plan on the hood of Lamar's car: who would do what, and who would be where. There would be close to forty law enforcement personnel taking part. Every one would have a specific job. The sheriff's department was put in charge of all potential escape routes, including entries and exits for I-40 and farther up on Route 66. They would all have to be sealed off. It was his job to make sure his deputies got into position and played containment if they had to. Lamar referred to them as the defensive backs.

The Kingman police would supply the backup muscle for the agents. They would be on site and potentially in direct contact with the suspects. It was their job to prevent the sheriff's crew from having to make tackles. Lamar referred to them as the linebackers. Galey took particular interest in the name since that was his position on the

Arizona State football team back in the day. Almost forty years had passed. Memories though were still as vivid as the limp from his deteriorating left hip. An injury from his playing days before the Bulldogs became the Sun Devils. A name change he never grew fond of.

The agents would enter the room: the front line of the assault. The risk was always great. Fully aware of the suspects' violent history, it was likely they were armed. They wouldn't go willingly. The agents' advantage, though, would be surprise and the use of overwhelming force. If they could gain quick entry into the small room, then they could possibly reach the suspects before they had a chance to react. Before they had a chance to reach for their weapons and use them. A motel room was one of the best places to capture a suspect because of its size. A home or apartment presented many more obstacles with their multiple rooms.

Daybreak was close to six o'clock, and the assault on room eighteen would take place at seven, an hour after the family in room twenty-one checked out quietly at the direction of the FBI. The Seyferts would also be moved off property. That could be done easily from where their living quarters were. Far enough away from room eighteen not to raise suspicion, or even be seen or heard. The biggest gamble was with the truckers. Some of whom may even head back out onto the road before sunrise. But that was all normal life for them and those who stayed at motels like the Saturn. Truckers came and went at all hours of the day and night. Their coming and going wouldn't raise any eyebrows.

They reviewed the plan several times, making some minor changes. Everyone was on the same page. It would be a long night of waiting.

Rosalie Gonzales was picked up at her home by Sheriff Jackson at four in the morning. She was waiting on the front porch of her small ranch house that looked like everyone else's in her neighborhood. A fifties development of one-story ranch homes for the middle class.

She was a short, somewhat stocky Hispanic woman in her late forties: a twelve-year veteran of the sheriff's department. She loved her job. Never complained. Worked holidays and overtime when needed. She was divorced and was the mother of twin girls who were grown and living with their own families in Texas and New Mexico. The phone call from her boss at two in the morning had caught her by surprise, but it wasn't the first time she had been summoned in the middle of the night to perform her duties as a deputy.

Jackson had filled her in on what was going down at the Saturn. It was the opportunity of a lifetime for Rose. She asked few questions and was willing and able to do whatever they needed, no matter the danger. Jackson appreciated her willingness and told her what time to be ready.

The two drove to the rendezvous at an empty car dealership lot. Gonzales was further briefed along the way.

Once there she was given several photographs of the male suspect by Agent Lamar and an artist's rendition of the female suspect.

"Study them carefully, Rose," Jackson told her as she sat in the front seat of the sheriff's unmarked car. The inside overhead light was on, and a flashlight was firmly gripped in her hand. "What you can't see is his size. He's every bit of six foot two and muscular."

It was their hope that he may come to the door when she knocked on it. Get him out of bed early in the morning. That would give her an easy way to identify him. If he stayed in bed and the female occupant answered the door, then it would be tougher for Gonzales.

"Deputy Gonzales, whenever you're ready just let me know, and we'll head over there," Agent Lamar leaned down and said through Jackson's open window.

"I'm ready anytime you are, sir," she told him.

She said good-bye to Jackson and then got out and followed Lamar over to his car. The two of them got in. They drove down the road to the Saturn and pulled into the motel like guests. They parked just behind the office, where there was an exit and entry into the Seyferts' living quarters. Ruth greeted them. Eugene made their acquaintance as well.

"It's a pleasure to meet you, Ruth and Eugene," Lamar said to the Seyferts. "On behalf of the entire FBI, I can't thank you enough for all that you've done."

"There's no need to thank us. We're just doing what any other responsible citizens would do," Ruth replied, and then she turned to Gonzales. "When Agent Lamar called me a few hours ago and told me what was taking place, I rounded up several housekeeping uniforms for you. I have them over here if you'd like to try them on," she said, and then she made her way over to a small closet where motel supplies were kept. Mostly linens and bedding.

Deputy Gonzales found one that looked to be about her size and then went into the bedroom and tried it on. The bulletproof vest that Lamar had brought for her went on first. The uniform fit. Not perfectly, but good enough. She came back out, and Lamar gave his approval. So did the Seyferts. Ruth took her around to the front office and showed her the housekeeping cart stacked with linens, towels, and cleaning supplies. Standing next to it, Gonzales looked the part.

She and Lamar went through one last rehearsal, and then he shook her hand and said good luck. He glanced out at the "No Vacancy" sign that he had instructed Ruth to turn on to keep traffic to a minimum. It was highly visible. He handed Gonzales the portable two-way radio and she put it behind the counter. She was to use it to call him after she identified the suspects and returned to the office.

"Ruth and Eugene, please follow me," he instructed the Seyferts.

The three of them exited through the door in the living quarters and got into Lamar's car. He drove them to an awaiting car, which he had arranged to take them out of harm's way. The transfer was made, and then Lamar met up with Kerrigan and the others back at the vacant dealership.

"Game on, let's go," he said to the men, and then the heavily armed group got into their cars and drove off to take up their positions near the motel. All waiting for the call from Deputy Gonzales.

As the sun rose upon the city of Kingman, it cast a sliver of light on the roofline of the Saturn Motel. Like the shiny edge of a knife. Deputy Gonzalez opened the office door and began her stroll down the concrete walkway that led to all the rooms of the motel. It was elevated a few inches above the parking lot. The housekeeping cart's wheels squeaked, but could barely be heard over the air conditioners that were running in the truckers' rooms she passed. Sweat in her armpits dripped down her sides. Room eighteen was quickly coming up.

When Gonzales was a few steps from it, the door opened and its guest Andrea Bennett exited, shutting the door behind her. She didn't even look at Gonzales. She got into her car. Thinking quickly, Gonzales held up a towel in her attempt to be let into the room. Andrea Bennett shook her head no and then backed up and turned to leave the motel grounds. She took a right onto the road heading toward central Kingman. At the intersection one thousand feet from the motel the light turned red and she stopped; she started to wind her window down to have a smoke. Before she even brought her eyes back up from the purse with the cigarettes in it sitting next to her on the front seat of the Impala, four cars pulled up on each side of her, effectively blocking her from going anywhere, and then eight men with guns drawn swarmed around her demanding, "Put your hands in the air. Off the steering wheel, now! Get them up where we can see them. Now! Do it now!"

They had Bonnie. It was time to capture Clyde.

CHAPTER FORTY-THREE

I worked twelve- and fourteen-hour days waiting for Erin to come back for New Year's Eve. It seemed easier to wait for her in Aspen than it did in NYC. Maybe it was the shortened geographical distance that made things easier. Or just being in our apartment with her stuff. Her paintings. The bed we shared. Whatever it was, I knew I had made the right decision to get out of Manhattan. I would make it up to my parents another time.

The day before New Year's Eve, I worked late getting some skis prepared for a family who had given me a big tip to make sure everything was ready for them in the morning. They had just arrived from Austria, and their own skis had gotten lost on their flight. Our store was their best option since we always stayed open an hour longer than our competitors. New skis, bindings, and poles for the husband, wife, and two kids. I had suggested they rent skis until their skis arrived from their airline, but money wasn't an object, so they chose to buy. After I had informed him that since we were a few minutes from closing that it might not be until noon the next day that we would have things ready for him, he put a hundred-dollar bill in front of me to make sure his family could hit the lifts with their new equipment at eight in the morning.

It was around ten o'clock when I made it back to the apartment. The long day had caught up with me. I plopped onto the couch with a beer and the smell of a frozen pizza cooking in the oven. My feet were tired, and I put them onto the coffee table. Looking around, I saw a few things that needed to be straightened up or put away before Erin arrived the next afternoon. She would appreciate coming home to a somewhat clean-looking place. I would do it in the morning. It could wait. The couch had tackled me, and I wasn't going anywhere. The only disappointment being that I'd forgotten to grab two beers out of the fridge instead of one, which when finished would require legwork.

The phone rang. It was too early to be Erin, who always called me around midnight, so I just let it ring. I didn't feel like being bothered. Some guys at work were meeting up at Little Nell's, and it was probably just them trying to get me to come out. It eventually stopped ringing. A moment later it rang again. They were persistent. I got up and walked over to the phone that was by the kitchen. The beer still in my hand. I would kill two birds with one stone and make a trip to the fridge along the way. I answered, and to my surprise it was Erin.

"Hey, Alex," she said in a less-than-casual way.

"Mr. Cavanaugh speaking," I replied to let her know we were less than a day away from seeing each other and there was no reason to be serious. She forced a laugh. "You're early tonight. Didn't you go out?"

"My mom and dad took all of us out for dinner, and I didn't feel like meeting up with my friends afterward. Did you do anything? "

"I was slammed at work and just got home a few minutes ago." I took a sip of my fresh beer and sat down on one of the two stools at the counter that separated the kitchen from the dining room.

There was an odd silence. We'd had a few of them during our phone conversations when I was in NYC, but being back home in Aspen brought expectations of being perfectly comfortable with each other. At least from my end.

"Hey, I've changed my flight," she said, breaking the silence.

"So what time are you coming in tomorrow?" I held the phone a little bit tighter to my ear. More silence.

"I'm not. I'm staying in LA for a few more days." It was definitely a big letdown. I rubbed my hand through my hair and put my elbows on the counter.

"I was hoping we could spend New Year's Eve together, but it looks like we don't feel the same about that," I said, letting her hear my disappointment. "Hang on a second, I've got to get the pizza out of the oven. I can smell it starting to burn." It would give me time to think.

I put down the phone and grabbed the hand towel by the sink and pulled the pizza tray out of the oven, leaving it on top of the stove for it to cool. "OK, I'm back. Not much of a cook am I?"

"No, that you definitely aren't."

"Why aren't you coming home tomorrow? How will I keep the girls off of me when the clock strikes midnight?" I said, throwing in some humor to mask the hurt I felt inside.

"The ocean is good for me. Same as you and your snow. So maybe forget to brush your teeth tomorrow and skip the deodorant. That should help with the girls."

There was the temptation to keep the game of matching wits going, but it wouldn't serve a purpose. I changed tones.

"OK, no more jokes. Seriously, Erin, what's going on?"

She let out a long sigh, as if she'd been holding it in for days. "Honestly, I don't know how I feel about you anymore. About us." I could sense the relief she felt getting those words out.

"It's been a long time coming, hasn't it?"

"Yes," she said. A solid, long, drawn-out yes followed by a long silence between us. Longer than the previous ones.

"But I know how I feel about you, and how I want us to be," I said. "And I know I screwed things up." Without seeing her eyes there was no reason to say any more. It would be better to wait until she got back to Aspen to scratch below the surface.

More silence. Neither of us knowing what came next. She eventually gave me her new flight times for her arrival on Thursday night and I told her I'd be at the airport to pick her up. We discussed our possible New Year's Eve plans, agreeing to give each other the night off then from having to be home by a certain time to call each other. It could wait until the following morning. At the end of the call, we simply said good-bye. Nothing more.

CHAPTER FORTY-FOUR

Kerrigan pulled her out of the car, cuffed her, frisked her, and threw her into the back of his car. The one Lamar had been driving. Two of the other agents got in the back with Kaylee, and they sped off to their command center at the dealership. All the cars followed them again. When they got there, Lamar parked the car in the rear of the lot that was farthest from the street. Away from people and traffic. A place the rising sun had yet awakened. He turned around and looked at her from the front seat. The artist's rendering of her in his hand, and his eyes going back and forth from it to her like a ricochet. Several times. Everyone quiet. And waiting.

"She's our girl," he said to his fellow agents. "Get her out."

They took her out of the car and stood her up against the rear fender. Kerrigan kept a firm grip on one of her arms and the other two agents on the other side of her. She wasn't going anywhere.

"I'm Agent Russ Lamar of the Federal Bureau of Investigation, and you're being held in connection with the murder of Mark Dempsey and the kidnapping and felonious assault of Ellie Dempsey. You are also being held for the murders of Ranger Walt Edmonds, Sarah Evans, Clayton Binns, Gregory Langtim, and Florencio Munoz," he said, and then he read her Miranda Rights to her. "What's your name?"

"You have the wrong lady, mister," the woman replied.

"I asked you a question. What's your name?"

One of the agents had her purse, which didn't have any identification in it. He kept looking at the various items in it hoping to find something.

"You look awfully sweet, holding my purse," she said. Kerrigan tightened his grip on her arm. "You're hurting me."

"I bet you heard those same words from Ellie Dempsey and Sarah Evans," Kerrigan said, and he squeezed even tighter.

"I don't know who you're talking about, and I want to see a lawyer."

Lamar took a step closer to her, and she saw his demeanor change. She knew his gloves were coming off. Several more cars turned into the old dealership lot and pulled up next to the group. Galey and Jackson with several of their men adding to the number of law enforcement personnel surrounding the suspect. As tough as Kaylee was, their numbers were beginning to intimidate her, a good thing for Lamar. Good timing.

"I'll get you to a lawyer if that's what you want, and then I can get back to doing my job. But let me tell you something first. My job is to apprehend—or if necessary, shoot to kill—those responsible for murdering five innocent people and I intend to continue doing that in a few minutes. And it's my belief that our other suspect, Lowell Henderson, is right now in room eighteen of the Saturn Motel."

Lamar walked around to the trunk of the car and pulled out a pump shotgun and an automatic rifle, sinister-looking weapons. Several other agents opened their trunks and pulled out similar weapons. In no time they resembled a platoon ready for battle. Lamar said, "Knowing your scumbag accomplice like I do, he's not going to go quietly. And frankly, I don't care. I'd just as soon put a bullet through his head from forty feet away than go through the hassle of trying to take him alive and splitting my lip."

"I love target practice, and that piece of shit of yours is one big target," added Kerrigan. "I'd like nothing more than to splatter his head all over that motel room." He smiled at her with an evil on the side of good that she had never before encountered.

One of the agents took a call in his car and then came back to the group. He informed Lamar and the others that the family in room twenty-one were off the motel grounds. Kaylee stood there remaining silent. Defiant.

"You know what that means," Lamar said to her. "Now we don't have to worry about stray bullets. We're just going to go over there, give him one opportunity to surrender peacefully, and if he doesn't comply, which I hope he doesn't, then we're going to pump that shitty little motel room with so much tear gas his eyes will literally catch on fire. Then he'll blindly come storming out of the room, and we'll fill him up with so much lead he could qualify as a giant number two pencil. So when you said goodbye to him this morning on your way to getting coffee or wherever the hell you were going, be advised that was the last time you saw him alive. Think about that for a second before I hand you over to the sheriff, who can take you to your jail cell and call you a lawyer."

Lamar turned away from her and walked over to the car next to his. He reached in through the open window and pulled out a handful of shotgun shells and dumped them into the side pocket of his FBI-issued navy-blue windbreaker. Company letters in yellow on the back. He turned his attention back to the woman and opened the chamber of the shotgun by pulling down on the forearm. The shell went in, and then he quickly and loudly slammed the chamber shut by extending the forearm, the unmistakable sound of a pump-action shotgun being loaded.

"Boys, let's go hunt this son of a bitch," Lamar said, and then he started to turn for the driver's door and the other agents for theirs. "Sheriff, she's all yours."

"Don't you hurt my Lowell," the woman screamed as Sheriff Jackson began taking her to his cruiser. Lamar stopped and the other agents did too. His tactics had worked.

"Sheriff, just a second," Lamar said. The sheriff and his deputy stopped for him. Lamar walked over to them with his agents in tow.

"This is the last time I'm going to ask you. What's your name?"

"Kaylee Ryland, and I'll tell you what you want to know. Just don't hurt my Lowell," she said, her lower lip was quivering.

Working quickly, they got all the information they needed. The weapons in the room. That Lowell was in the room alone. When he expected her back. In an attempt to save Lowell's life, Kaylee confessed to everything they had done and began to go into detail of all their abhorrent crimes.

"Please don't hurt my baby," she pleaded with Lamar. He looked at her with disgust and didn't answer. "I'll tell the sheriff everything. Bring my baby back," she said to Lamar as Jackson loaded her into the cruiser, slamming the door.

They surrounded the motel and positioned themselves so that if Lowell Henderson took one step out of the door he would be in the line of fire from every direction. They shielded themselves with their cars, and a few of the men took up sniper positions on the roof of the single-story motel. One agent crouched behind a truck tire.

"Lowell Henderson, this is Agent Russ Lamar of the FBI. Put down your weapons and come out with your hands above your head. Kaylee Ryland is in our custody." He kept it as close to the FBI handbook as possible, almost word for word. The bullhorn was turned up all the way. He looked at his watch, and after fifteen seconds he said the same thing again and added, "You have sixty seconds to comply." He neglected to say anything about being completely surrounded or going into any detail about the massive amount of firepower that was trained on room eighteen. It would be just as easy to shoot him as it would be to go through the long and expensive process of a trial and an execution after years and years of appeals. Lamar and Kerrigan were ready and willing to bring justice for Lowell Henderson's victims as swiftly as possible. They were sworn to protect and serve, and they could think of no better way of dealing with the beast they had finally cornered at the Saturn Motel than by putting him down.

At the sixty-second mark, the power to the motel was cut and the first canister of tear gas was fired through the window and curtain next to the air-conditioning unit that had fallen silent. Seconds later, Lamar gave the order to fire the second can of tear gas into the room. All the agents waited. Weapons trained on the window and door. The irritant dispersed and filled the room, pouring out of the shattered window. The door flew open. Lowell Henderson attempted to gasp fresh air while remaining on the floor of the room. Hidden below the window with a wet towel pressed against his freshly shaved face. A revolver in his hand. A shotgun on the floor next to him. Shirtless with just his jeans on.

"You have ten seconds to come out with your hands up," Lamar said through the bullhorn, glancing at the second hand of his watch.

Lowell reached around into the doorway and began firing his revolver wildly, not looking at what he was shooting. His head and body was behind the wall and underneath the window. After his first shot, a hail of armor-piercing bullets from automatic rifles and handguns as well as buckshot from twelve-gauge shotguns ripped into the hollow-block of room eighteen of the Saturn Motel. Many high-powered rifle shots penetrated the room, and three of them hit Lowell Henderson in the torso, leg, and foot. They heard him wailing like a wounded hound.

Kerrigan kept his high-powered assault rifle trained on the room. The sight on his gun looking for a head shot somewhere near the doorway behind the wall. He fired four shots in quick succession. The wailing stopped.

Cautiously, Kerrigan came out from behind the car and slowly approached the motel, his assault rifle drawing a bead on the window and doorway. Back and forth. His shoulders hunched. Right foot leading the way with each step and then the left coming forward. A continuous shooting stance. As he neared the doorway, he saw an outstretched hand holding a revolver on the floor of the room. It looked lifeless. Two more steps confirmed it was. Lowell Henderson's body lay in a pool of blood.

The upper right half of the man's head was shattered from Kerrigan's bullets. He lowered his weapon, and that was the signal to everyone else that it was over.

When Kaylee was informed of Lowell's death, they put her on suicide watch at the Mohave County Jail. She was to remain there until her transfer to Phoenix, who had put claims on her first. Oregon and California were to follow. But neither would ever occur.

It was never determined how she managed to get a hold of the razor blade that she used to slash her wrists, especially an inmate on suicide watch, and why it took the guards so long to realize what she had done. It was speculated that they let her have her way, to simply let her end her life so that the families of her victims could get on with theirs. The truth was never known, nor pursued vigorously.

CHAPTER FORTY-FIVE

It was a long few days. Too many beers and hangovers, and work. Late nights lying in bed alone. Wondering. I did my best to stay busy. Not think about Erin. It wasn't easy. I bought a new car and traded mine in to help pass the time. A used 1979 Toyota FJ40. Burnt-sienna with black interior. I had always wanted one. Perfect for the mountains. A compulsive buy, but one I didn't regret.

Thursday came and I left work and headed out to Sardy Field at six o'clock. Erin's connecting flight from Denver was due in at six thirty. Light snow had begun falling. It gradually increased, my headlights magnifying it. The windshield wipers were on medium speed as I traveled at forty miles per hour down Highway 82. The airport wasn't the easiest of airports to fly in or out of, especially with low visibility, so I knew there was a chance her flight would be delayed or they'd land at a nearby airport and shuttle them up to Aspen on a bus. As much as I always prayed for snow, I wanted it to stop.

When I reached the terminal, one of the attendants said her flight was on time. I took a seat and looked out for the incoming lights of the plane. I was nervous. Wetness in the pit of my arms. I knew it wasn't an easy thing to fly a plane and land it on a small strip of land surrounded by mountains in a snowstorm.

Adding to my anxiety was that Erin and I would also have to finish where we left off.

It looked like a Broadway marquee all lit up when the plane appeared through the snow. Coming out of no-where and then touching down. An amazing bit of flight-craft. The United Airlines insignia barely visible on the turboprop as it taxied toward me and the few other people who had joined me in the terminal. Some of my nervous-ness was replaced with excitement. Though it had only been ten days since I had last seen Erin, it felt more like a month. Or longer. The plane and its propellers came to a stop. A minute later the door opened and the steps unfolded leading down to the tarmac. She was the fourth person off the plane. The fifth was Kelley Alston, whom I wasn't expecting to see.

They were covered in snow by the time they came into the terminal. I said hello to Kelley and mentioned that I hoped she was doing better. Dealing with Carter's death was hard on her. I wrapped my arms around Erin. The reunion would've been more personal, but I played it cool with Kelley around.

"Welcome home," I said to Erin.

I turned to Kelley. "Here to do some skiing? Looks like you timed it right." I gestured to the falling snow outside. "How was your flight?" I said to both of them.

"No problem from LA to Denver, but then they almost cancelled our flight from there because of the snow," said Erin. "I called you at the apartment to let you know, but you didn't answer."

"I worked today and came directly from there."

"Oh, I should've tried you there. I thought you were off today for some reason."

"I was supposed to be, but we had a guy quit, and I came in to help out," I said, and then turned to Kelley in her full-length white down coat with a fur-lined collar that matched the fur on the tops of her Sorel boots. Her long blond hair was pulled back in a ponytail, wet from the melting snow.

"So how have you been doing?" I asked. It had been several months since I'd seen her. She had come into town briefly after Carter's death. She and Erin were close. They were always there for each other in tough times, and that's why her presence had me a little on guard. Especially since Erin had not told me she was coming.

Their bags were delivered, and then I carried them out to my car. Erin loved the new wheels. I knew she would, but that was only a minor reason for buying it. I drove Kelley to

Megan's place. That's where she was going to stay while in town. Erin had arranged it. There was much more room there than our place, and I knew that Erin was thinking of the two of us. We had some things to work out, and it would be tough with Kelley staying with us. Dropping Kelley off made me feel more at ease with her arrival. Not such a big deal after all.

We got back to our apartment, and I grabbed a beer for me and a glass of wine for Erin. We sat down on the couch. Legs stretched out onto the coffee table, I put my arm around her. She leaned into me.

"Cheers," I said, and our drinks kissed. The glass doors to our balcony across from us revealed the winter wonderland occurring under the watchful eye of our neighbor's floodlight. "Are you still trying to figure out how you survived ten days without me?" Erin looked up at me with her blue eyes and her crooked smile. I could tell she still loved me. A part of me. Something was still there.

"When do you want to talk?" she said, letting me know that as much as she loved my humor, we needed to finish what we had begun on the phone the other night. We both knew it was coming.

"Now is as good a time as any. I have you booked for a fifty-minute session. I'll just need to make a copy of your insurance card."

She smiled again. Those amazing eyes.

"No listen, I mean it. We have to talk. Okay?" She took her thumb and finger and grabbed my skin just below my rib cage.

"OK, OK, ouch." I squirmed out of her grasp. Then right back together on the couch.

"I've been doing a lot of thinking, Alex. I guess that's what happens when you hang at home with your parents for too long."

"So it wasn't so good being back in LA?"

"LA was great, but being back home and having to tip-toe around my parents at times was a drag. I completely forgot what living at home was like. It's been so long, I guess."

"Tell me what you thought about."

"Us," she replied.

"What about us?"

She turned a little so that she was more facing me than the glass doors. I did the same. The snow would have to wait.

"I just can't get past what happened. When I think of you—and yes, I love you, Alex—there is this scar though, and I'm convinced it's never going to completely go away. It's like you and Carter were leading this double life or something with all the lies. That you would do something that would jeopardize our relationship makes me wonder if I can ever trust you. And that there is this other side of you that I never knew was there is definitely a question mark. I'm just being honest."

"It was a mistake, Erin. I've apologized a million times to you. And there's no double life or anything like that. And please don't put me in the same category as Carter. Yes, I lied to you, and I regret it from the bottom of my heart. I will never lie to you again. I promise. You just have to believe me and trust me."

"That's just it. You're asking me to do something that I'm not sure I can do."

"What do you mean?"

"You're saying I need to trust you after you spent two months lying to me. And look at everything that happened. I can't just wipe the slate clean and go on pretending everything is great between us. It doesn't work that way. At least not for me."

"I'm not asking you to do that. I know I can't wave a magic wand and make everything like it used to be. But if you give it some time, give us some time, I will do everything I can to put things back together," I said sincerely as we looked each other in the eyes. Our drinks on our laps.

The snow came back into view for both of us. So bright as it reflected off the floodlight. Like tinsel. It was coming down hard, and I saw myself at the top of Highlands. My favorite place to ski in Aspen. First tracks. Maroon Bells in the distance. It was always an easy escape.

"I'll build a fire," I said, and I got up and threw some logs into the fireplace.

"I'm moving back to LA, Alex."

I turned from the fireplace where I was squatting to place the last log on the grate. I let go of it and wiped my hands. Her legs came off the coffee table, and she drew them up underneath herself. Indian style. I picked my beer up and sat back down next her. But unlike her I faced the snow. I felt wounded, and for a moment I just sat there licking my wounds.

"When did you decide this?" I kept looking at the snow. Hypnotized by it. Or trying to be.

"I've been thinking about it for a while. This is your world. You love the mountains, the snow, the skiing, the fishing. You belong here. And I like it here, but I don't love it. I came here to be with you."

"So why don't you stay?"

"Because I want the ocean and the sun and warm air, and I want to follow my dream—and this isn't the place to do it."

I knew she was referring to her painting, and that was something I never wanted to hold her back from. But I also knew that it wasn't really the geography but more with her falling out of love with me. The part about the scar not healing and the slate not being able to be wiped clean.

"Did you meet someone while you were home?" I asked, making sure I wasn't missing something.

"Come on, do you really have to ask that?"

"Just checking."

"If you want to come with us, you're more than welcome. But I'm not promising anything. I'm willing to give things a try there, but I don't want to live together."

"Who is us?" I asked her.

"Kelley is going to drive back with me."

"So that's why Kelley came here," I said, putting togeth-er the pieces of the puzzle. She had everything planned out. "Have you told your work?"

"I called them today, and my last day is next Wednesday."

"You haven't wasted any time," I replied, showing some of my hurt, and I drank the last of my beer. I got up and went to the fridge for another one, and I brought the bot-tle of wine too. I filled her glass. "I'm pretty sure you know this all comes as a shock for me. I mean you could've told me what you were thinking at least. Maybe I don't know you as well as I thought."

"Maybe that goes for both of us."

"Be real. You know what I'm saying."

"You're not the only one dealing with this. Don't you think this is really tough for me too? I've been struggling with all of this for a while. You know how things have been. Some nights I can't sleep. And it's not any easier on me try-ing to work through all this when there are days we come home from work and barely talk to each other. It's like we're strangers. It sucks."

It was a long night. We drank into the late hours and watched the incredible snowstorm. Logs continuously put on the fire. We talked of everything, good times and bad. And we laughed. It was the way we used to be. She planned to leave the following Sunday. She would fit all her clothes and easel and paintings in her Jeep. She didn't want any of the furniture. Not that we had anything of value. She didn't want me to be without anything.

I couldn't follow her to LA. It wasn't the right thing for me. For either of us. Maybe time away from each other would be good. What was meant to be was meant to be. She would know how to find me, and I would know how to find her. It was around four in the morning when we cuddled up on the couch and closed our eyes. I had never felt closer to her.

CHAPTER FORTY-SIX

On that Sunday morning I got up early and went out and checked Erin's Jeep: the tires, oil, the battery cables. I gave it a test ride and then filled it up with gas at the station in Snowmass. When I got back she was up. Coffee in hand. Her morning ritual. I told her where I had been, and she gave me a kiss on the cheek. All of her clothes were put in big, dark-green plastic garbage bags to maximize shipping capacity; they sat in the hallway. I loaded them one by one into the car, leaving a little space for Kelley's suitcase. After they were packed, I put her easel on top of them and then her paintings last. She left me with my two favorites of hers.

She showered, and I finished loading up a few odds and ends. The goal was to fit everything into the back of the Jeep, and I accomplished that. Her rearview mirror was blocked by everything stacked up so high, which I didn't like, but there was no way around it. I offered to ship some of her things to her, but she insisted she'd be fine.

I leaned against the bed and watched her get dressed. She was so beautiful. And she looked at me from time to time as she blew dry her hair in the full-length mirror that was attached to the bedroom closet door. No words between us. Just our eyes.

When she finished she called Kelley and told her she was on her way. I told her the weather looked good all the way to LA and that she shouldn't have any problems. If she did, I was just a phone call away. We walked out to her car in the early-morning light. The cold. We stopped together at the driver's door. I hugged her and told her I'd always love her. "Me too," she replied, and then she got into the car.

She slowly drove away. I stood there until she went out of view.

CHAPTER FORTY-SEVEN

The first night without her was not much different than the one I spent alone up in the mountains when Sarah died. And the ones that followed didn't get any easier. That was how the remainder of winter went. A routine of immersing myself in work preceded by nights of tossing and turning until the sun would arrive, allowing me to do the same on skis for an hour or two before sliding my time card into the clock. The few friends I had provided an outlet every once in a while when we'd meet up at the Paragon or Red Onion for beers and far too many shots of Jäger, and sometimes I'd run into Megan which seemed to help pass the time, but nothing filled the void from losing Erin.

When Spring rolled in and the lifts came to a halt right after Easter weekend, I found myself in a town that was quickly being abandoned. Like Middlebury at the end of May. The start of the off-season. Prevailing winds of mud and slush while the mountains shed their skin and the rivers carried it away. All in the preparation for the new life of summer. Life containing the fly and trout that held equal status to the fly fisherman since he needed both to pursue his passion.

I had grown tired of the misery, and the waiting. As I have said, I was never much good at it. I would rather climb out of the ceiling of the stuck elevator and up the shaft than put my hopes in a rescue. My rescue wasn't coming. I was convinced of that.

On the third Saturday morning of April, I sat down at the kitchen counter with a new Rand McNally road atlas trying to figure out where to go after loading up my FJ40 with camping and fishing gear. Putting the cart before the horse. I did that sometimes. Studying the map revealed an endless number of choices. I had yet to see the Grand Canyon. North was Jackson Hole and Yellowstone. Northwest was the Alaska Highway and the last frontier. More trout, salmon and steelhead streams than could possibly be fished in a lifetime. But I was only fooling myself with imaginary adventures that, at best, would be nothing more than a Band-Aid over the root cause of my sorrow, which were Erin and Sarah. As many times as I had awakened in the middle of the night with the sunken feeling of what I had done to Erin and our relationship, there was an almost equal number of times when I would lay there thinking about what I hadn't done for Sarah's family and her husband.

It clearly wasn't enough to leave them with a one-page letter outlining her misfortunes and what she and I had done in an attempt to reverse them. It wasn't fair or morally right to let them go through the rest of their lives with the words I had typed on a sheet of paper as her final words spoken from the grave. She had much more to tell them.

Crossing the bridge over Maroon Creek always brought mixed emotions. The front door to Aspen. Out I went. There was mist that had a chance of becoming rain or snow and I turned my wipers on periodically to clear the windshield as I drove along Highway 82. The forecast called for the possibility of sunshine later in the day, but I wouldn't be around for it if it came.

I pulled into the gas station when I reached Carbondale. No particular reason other than it felt like an old friend I wanted to say goodbye to and support with the purchase of some cokes and peanut-butter crackers for the journey. As I continued traveling on 82 into the lower elevations of the Roaring Fork Valley, the mist was breaking up and I could see the faint image of the sun appearing above the mountains. It was slightly brighter than the pale-grey of the overcast sky. A solid white circle like an aspirin. I reached over for my sunglasses and put them on.

The town of Glenwood Springs was the junction of four directions and the rivers and highways that went with them. The Roaring Fork River and Highway 82 traveled north and south. The Colorado River and I-70 went east and west. I slowed down for the traffic light just before the bridge over to the interstate, and came to a stop. I opened up the road atlas and looked at Laramie. I then flipped the pages to California— Northern and Southern. Back to Laramie. The light turned green and I shifted into gear.

ABOUT THE AUTHOR

Into the Roaring Fork is Jeff Howe's first novel and has received positive reception across the Midwest and Rocky Mountain West. He is near completion on his second novel. Jeff is a Cincinnatian, born in 1963, the son of James and Marjorie Howe and the youngest of nine children. He was raised Catholic and attended Catholic grade and high school. In 1985 he graduated from the University of Cincinnati.

Upon graduation he moved to Aspen, Colorado where he worked for KSPN radio station. When the ski season ended he moved to Los Angeles for a brief period and then returned to Cincinnati where he went to work for his family's business, a manufacturer and distributor of process heating elements and temperature sensors used in the plastics industry. After a few years he grew restless and left the company to travel and pursue other interests. Eventually settling down, he rejoined the family business, married, fathered two children, and lives with his wife and kids in Cincinnati.

An avid fly fisherman of both freshwater and saltwater game fish, Jeff has a true passion for being connected to the water, and attempts to do so every chance he gets. In addition to his outdoor pursuits, which also include hunting, he plays piano and guitar.

www.jeffhowebooks.com